TALL, DARK AND SEXY
The men who never fail—seduction included!

Brooding, successful and arrogant, these
men have a dangerous glint in their eye and
can sweep any female they desire off her
feet. But now there's only one woman each
man wants—and each will use their wealth,
power, charm and irresistibly seductive
ways to claim her!

Don't miss any of the titles in
this exciting collection:

The Billionaire's Virgin Bride
Helen Brooks

His Mistress by Marriage
Lee Wilkinson

The British Billionaire Affair
Susanne James

The Millionaire's Marriage Revenge
Amanda Browning

SUSANNE JAMES has enjoyed creative writing since childhood, completing her first—sadly unpublished—novel by the age of twelve. She has three grown-up children who were, and are, her pride and joy, and who all live happily in Oxfordshire with their families. She was always happy to put the needs of her family before her ambition to write seriously, although along the way some articles published for magazines and newspapers helped to keep the dream alive!

Susanne's big regret is that her beloved husband is no longer here to share the pleasure of her recent success. She now shares her life with Toffee, her young Cavalier King Charles spaniel, who decides when it's time to get up (early) and when a walk in the park is overdue!

THE BRITISH BILLIONAIRE AFFAIR

SUSANNE JAMES

~ TALL, DARK AND SEXY ~

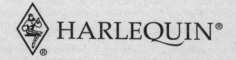

TORONTO • NEW YORK • LONDON
AMSTERDAM • PARIS • SYDNEY • HAMBURG
STOCKHOLM • ATHENS • TOKYO • MILAN • MADRID
PRAGUE • WARSAW • BUDAPEST • AUCKLAND

ISBN-13: 978-0-373-82351-2
ISBN-10:   0-373-82351-7

THE BRITISH BILLIONAIRE AFFAIR

First North American Publication 2008.

www.eHarlequin.com

Printed in U.S.A.

THE BRITISH
BILLIONAIRE AFFAIR

CHAPTER ONE

'CANDIDA—do come and sit here, next to me!' Rick Dawson pulled out a chair at the huge mahogany table for the girl to take her place, and she smiled gratefully, realising that she was unlikely to know anyone else at the party other than her hosts—Rick and his wife Faith. Although Candida was used to meeting strangers during the course of her work as an interior design consultant, social occasions were another matter entirely, and she always sent up a silent prayer to her guardian angel for support!

She could see at once that this was to be a fairly elaborate occasion, with everyone formally dressed. But the atmosphere was informal enough, and friendly chatting and laughing filled the large room. Candida was relieved to be sitting down to eat, rather than having to balance buffet food as well as holding a wine glass. Besides, the very high-heeled strappy shoes she'd chosen to wear were already beginning to pinch!

'In case you're all wondering,' Faith said to the assembled gathering, raising her voice above the chatter as she took her place at the other end of the table, 'we've got caterers doing the honours this evening. So there's no need for you all to ask me how I find the time to feed thirty of us *and* look after a two-year-old!'

Candida caught the woman's eye and they both smiled, a familiar look passing between them. On the few occasions that Faith had brought little Emily with her when she'd come to Farmhouse Cottage during all the refurbishments, work had tended to get held up! But at last everything, inside and out, had been completed on time, and this evening's party was to celebrate the fact.

Glancing up, Candida soon realised that the chair to her right was vacant. Someone had obviously cancelled at the last moment, she thought briefly.

Rick smiled down at her. 'What projects are you working on at the moment, Candida?' he asked, filling her glass to the brim. 'Still busy?'

'Nothing as big as this has been, Rick,' Candida replied truthfully. 'Just some small niggles on one contract to put right, and an enquiry to follow up.' The fact was, this extended fourteenth-century building, which the Dawsons had spent a lot of money bringing up to standard, had been one of the most valuable assignments that Candida had ever dealt with. And all her suggestions for the interior finishings had been instantly agreed upon. Faith—pretty, blonde and bubbly—had seemed relieved to let Candida take all the responsibility and initiative. From their very first meeting the two women had taken to each other straight away, and Faith's attitude to Candida was verging on the maternal, even though they were of a similar age, both being in their late twenties.

Presently, just as a young waitress appeared and began to serve them the first course, the sound of the front door slamming loudly made everyone stop talking briefly, and Faith looked up, feigning annoyance.

'Honestly! At last! Brothers are the most inconsiderate of guests! I *told* him not to be late, and he promised me that this time he'd be good!'

There was a general murmur of greeting, most seeming to know the latecomer who breezed into the room. The man went straight over to Faith and gave her a bear hug.

'Sorry, Faith—Rick—' The deep, masculine voice, sultry in manner, and as rich as dark chocolate melting on the tongue, resonated around the room. 'I got held up. Not my fault—honest!'

'It never is, is it, Maxy?' Faith said with mock sarcasm. 'Now, sit down by Candida and be sociable for once!'

So the empty seat next to her was for 'Maxy', Candida thought, glancing up at him as he pulled back his chair. He looked down at her briefly.

'Hi,' he said. 'I'm Max. I believe you're the woman of the moment—Ms Candida Greenway?'

'No. I'm Candy,' Candida corrected, feeling suddenly unexpectedly nervy—and apprehensive. Well, she'd not had much practice at meeting new men lately, she reminded herself, or been to many parties. To say nothing of the fact that she'd already drunk two glasses of very good wine on an empty stomach! Which could account for the sudden tremble of her hand as she reached for her glass!

He sat down, his tall, well-built frame only just managing to fit into the upholstered dining chair, and Candida looked up at him curiously. So this was Faith's brother. There was no resemblance between them, she thought—and Faith had never even mentioned him during their conversations. His rather long, glossy dark hair fell carelessly around his ears and the nape of his neck, falling forward over his forehead in a thick, unruly shock of waves, obviously with a life of their own, threatening to meet and overtake his well-defined eyebrows. As he looked back at her, Candida coloured up, her amber eyes responding instinctively to his sensuous inky-blue-black ones.

'I've heard all about you, you know,' he said matter-of-factly. 'My sister's been doing a wonderful PR job on your behalf.' He unfolded his napkin and placed it across his knees. 'From what she's been saying, you've taken all the responsibility from her—so good on you.' He smiled briefly, his teeth white against the colour of his tanned skin, but Candida had difficulty smiling back.

There was something about the man's attitude that was patronising and superior—two qualities she definitely did not like! And turning up so late was unforgivable, not to mention his obvious enjoyment at making an entrance. Slamming the door like that had been as effective as a roll of drums! She had definitely felt wary of him as soon as he'd sat down, his determined jaw and whole persona suggesting something of a brutish masculinity, and it had made her feel momentarily vulnerable. It was just rather unfortunate that he happened to be the most gorgeous man in the room! Not that *that* cut any ice with her! She reached forward again for her wine glass, and he immediately picked up his own, clinking it against hers.

'Good luck,' he said non-committally, as he took a generous mouthful. Then he turned to look at her again, assessing her appearance coolly, studying the heart-shaped face, tip-tilted nose and full lips. She was wearing a rather serious expression, he noticed, unless she suddenly showed her perfect white teeth, but her long chestnut hair, coiled high on the top of her head, must look wonderful left loose around her shoulders.

'D'you like these sort of affairs?' he said unexpectedly, and without waiting for a reply went on, 'Personally, I loathe them. But Faith and Rick's are always OK—the only ones I actually look forward to.' He picked up his knife and fork. 'I like the dress, by the way,' he said, almost as an afterthought. 'Colour's terrific. Suits you.'

Candida stared up at him blankly. She should have been pleased at the compliment, she thought, but for some reason it irritated her. They'd barely met, after all, and to her it felt out of place for him to pass any kind of judgement, good or otherwise, on what she was wearing. Even if it was the most expensive single item she'd ever purchased. It was fitted silk, with a flattering scoop neckline, the straight skirt just touching her knee. And the colour, a jewelled aquamarine shade, had reminded her instantly of sunlight on ocean waves.

Well, if she decided to be as familiar and outspoken as *he* was being, she could certainly air her own opinions! His round-necked, fine grey T-shirt—clearly exhibiting taut, well-toned chest muscles—casual pants and suede jacket, which he'd already slung carelessly over the back of his chair, hardly fitted the occasion. Every other man in the room was smartly dressed, and all were wearing ties. Instead, she decided to accept the compliment graciously.

'Thanks,' she said, equally casually. 'It was the colour which first attracted me…and fortunately it fitted as well.'

'Oh, it certainly does that,' he said at once, glancing down. 'You look as if you've been poured into it.'

That remark made Candida sit back hurriedly, suddenly self-conscious at his words. She knew it was rather revealingly low-cut, showing more cleavage than anything else she'd ever worn. And something in the way Faith's brother had made the point gave her the distinct impression that he was mentally undressing her!

Rick turned to her, interrupting them. 'I hope Max isn't being a nuisance,' he said, grinning over her head at his brother-in-law. 'He's an old cynic—don't let him intimidate you, Candida. He's got a reputation for eating delicious young women for lunch!'

Candida smiled back at Rick. 'I don't think I'd be quite to his taste,' she replied, saying the first thing that came into her head. 'And don't worry, Rick—I'm well able to look after myself.'

'I'm sure you are, Candida.' He paused, then spoke to Max. 'Why aren't we being graced by the lovely Ella's presence, then, Max? Faith said she wouldn't be coming tonight.'

'Oh, you know Ella. She has a way of letting me know when she's had enough of my company,' Max said evenly. 'So she's gone to spend a few days with Jack and Daisy—it'll be a bit of a change for her from the London scene. She sends her abject apologies, of course.'

After that, aided by fine food and good wine, Candida was aware that conversation seemed to flow quite easily. Max had a very clever way of shifting the emphasis on to her, and her life, while she was learning practically nothing about him. But what was obvious was that he adored his sister and small niece.

'I've always tended to be rather over-protective of Faith,' he admitted casually. 'She's twelve years younger than me, of course, which would explain it. But she was just about to do her Finals when our parents died unexpectedly, within a few months of each other. It proved to be a testing time.' He leaned forward to pass Candida a small jug of cream for her coffee, and the girl was struck by the way his eyebrows knitted darkly in a brief frown. They must have always been very close as a family, she thought instinctively.

'Well…I feel very fortunate that my father is alive and well,' she said slowly. 'And still living in the cottage where I was brought up.'

'And where's that?'

'Oh—an anonymous little village in South Wales.' She smiled, helping herself to sugar. 'But, sadly, my mother died when I was ten, and I don't think my father has ever really got over it.' She paused for a second or two, her expression clouding. 'I did try and take her place, and stayed at home for a while after college, but eventually I knew I had to get closer to London in order to succeed…it's where the money is. I think it's been the best thing for both of us, because my father seems to have made a real effort to go it alone…he's joined the local choir and goes on about it quite a lot! And because he's got more independent, I feel free to make my own way—though of course we're always chatting on the phone, and I visit as often as I can.'

There was silence for a moment or two, until he said suddenly, 'Where d'you live, and who with?'

The question was peremptory, and Candida bristled all over again. This man was *rude*! Was he a lawyer? Someone used to interrogating people? she thought. He certainly had a way of cutting to the chase! She set her lips in a straight line before replying.

'I live just outside Windsor—my flat is in a converted Victorian house in a rather boring street. And I don't live with anyone,' she added shortly, biting her lip. She'd parted company with Grant six months ago. They'd been a couple for more than a year, and the bitterness of their break-up was still raw and hurtful. She didn't want to be reminded of it.

'Um, well, that's a shame… There should be *someone* to zip you up into that dress,' Max said, glancing down at her, a faintly mocking smile on his lips.

'I'm perfectly capable of zipping myself up, thanks,' Candida said flatly.

She glanced up at him quickly, a faint blush beginning to slowly colour her fine olive skin. Making personal remarks was obviously something the man enjoyed, she thought.

Presently, the meal was over, and everyone moved away to wander off and talk to other people. For those who hadn't already done a tour of the house there was a chance for them to look around, and one or two drew Candida aside to talk shop, wanting to know which suppliers she usually used, where she'd obtained the fabulous limestone tiles in the bathrooms, and there were two requests for her to visit and suggest makeovers for their own places.

Faith had been right when she'd said there'd be a lot of interest at the party in her particular way of life,

Candida thought, though how much of it would actually come to definite assignments was another thing. She'd learned quite a lot about the fickleness of human nature, and aborted projects were not that unusual—especially after costs had been evaluated. But she was only too happy to answer all their queries.

During a lull, she looked around her and realised that the room was almost deserted. Her supper companion was certainly nowhere to be seen, and she shrugged inwardly. It was just like his type to shoot off at the first moment he could, she thought. Somehow, small talk and polite conversation didn't fit the persona she'd automatically labelled him with. Anyway, she was glad he'd gone, remembering again how he'd made her feel. Rick had described him as a cynic, and Candida sensed that the man was not the sort to suffer fools gladly. Not that she thought of herself as a fool, she reminded herself fiercely, but somehow she'd felt insignificant and beneath his estimation of who or what was important.

After a while, she excused herself from the small group still standing near, and went across the hall to Rick's study, which she knew would probably be empty. She needed a rest! She was definitely out of practice at these things, she thought. Why wasn't she at home now, safely tucked up under her lovely soft duvet?

Opening the door quickly, she went inside, shutting it noiselessly behind her, and without switching on the light moved over to Rick's huge armchair, which faced the window. Its plush high back gave no indication that anyone was already sitting there, but suddenly a deep voice said lazily, 'Ah—are you escaping too? Your

perfume has given you away, Candida. Come on—
there's room for both of us.'

Candida nearly jumped out of her skin, genuinely
shocked. 'Oh…I'm sorry…' she gasped. 'I didn't
know… I thought I'd be alone for a few moments…'

'My own idea exactly.' Max got up immediately, ges-
turing her towards him. 'Come on—your turn. This is
the best chair in the house, and I've already had a full
half-hour.'

As Candida hesitated, he moved across and pulled
her over so that she was forced to sit. She looked up,
seeing him more clearly now as she became more ac-
customed to the fading autumn light, conscious of his
eyes boring into her, of the determined mouth set in a
half-smile. She bent forward.

'I really must take these off,' she said. 'My feet are
killing me…' But before she could remove her shoes,
he'd knelt and casually slipped them both off.

'I think women deserve a medal for wearing these
sort of things,' he remarked off-handedly, turning them
over in his hands and examining them closely. 'Not
that they don't look good, of course—but don't they
cripple you?'

'Yes, sometimes,' Candida had to admit. 'But I
thought they went well with the…'

'With the dress? Yes, I'd second that.'

Candida leaned her head back against the chair, and
suddenly, without warning, she felt the warmth of Max's
strong hands as, crouching down, he took each of her
feet in turn, massaging them gently but firmly—almost
roughly. It was utter bliss, and she couldn't help giving
a long sigh of relief—and pleasure. '*Ohhhhh*—that's

wonderful,' she breathed, hating the thought that she was enjoying it! 'Where did you learn to do *that*?'

He didn't make any comment, and she let him continue for several moments, conscious of the dark head bent to the task, of his tanned, sensitive, manipulative fingers. Then he pressed his thumbs strongly under the soles of her feet, so that they were forced to arch beneath the pressure, and she gave a small cry of pleasurable pain. 'Ow!' she said, 'No—I mean, *oh*…that feels *so* good!'

He suddenly stopped what he'd been doing, and sat back on his heels.

Getting up, he moved across to the window and stared out over the garden, his hands thrust into his pockets. 'I envy my sister this house,' he said slowly. 'A wonderful place for Emily and any little sisters and brothers to be brought up.'

Candida stared across at him, wondering what sort of woman his wife was. From the comments he'd made to Rick earlier, Ella had a mind of her own—which was just as well, she thought. Because, to her, Max seemed an imperious, domineering member of the opposite sex—even though he'd done a pretty good job on her toes just now!

Suddenly the door was thrust open, and Rick came in.

'Seymour! There you are! I wondered where the hell you'd got to!' Then he noticed Candida, still curled up in his armchair. 'Oh—good, Candida. He's been looking after you, I hope? Come on—the brandy's being poured…'

But Candida was suddenly transfixed, unable to move a muscle. *What* had Rick just called his brother-in-law? *Seymour*? Was 'Maxy' the same person as Maximus Seymour of hated memory? For the next few moments Candida didn't hear a word of the conversation that was taking place over her head, as her thoughts, like crazy fireworks, stabbed at her consciousness in painful sparks. But, yes...*now* at last she recognised the man's face from the only time she'd ever seen it—once or twice, in a small inset photo in newspaper articles. No wonder she'd felt that surge of antagonism when she'd met him! It had been her spiritual sub-conscious alerting her!

Maximus Seymour, well-known writer and critic, whose mother before him had been a prolific author of biographies and historical novels. Candida had never been given the slightest hint about who Faith's family were, but, yes...looking up at the two men as they stood chatting, Candida recognised Maximus Seymour now, all right! Even if he did look older than his picture, which had obviously been taken some years before.

Practically shrinking back into the depths of the chair, Candida wondered how on earth she was going to get through the rest of this evening. In the fraction of a second everything had changed—for the worse! And now she wanted out!

Because, although they had never even met before this evening, Maximus Seymour had been solely responsible for robbing her—yes, *robbing* her—of her long-held desire, of her chance of a lifetime! And whatever happened to her, now or in the future, she knew she would resent it—resent *him*—for as long as she lived!

CHAPTER TWO

As EVERYONE started to gather again in the long, low-ceilinged sitting room, Candida excused herself and made her way along the hall to the cloakroom. Thankfully it was vacant, and she shut the door behind her, leaning against it for a moment. How on earth had fate brought her here, to cross the path of the man whose name, in her eyes, was mud?

Going over to the washbasin, she splashed cool water onto her reddened cheeks, dabbing them with one of the fluffy handtowels, then reached into her clutch bag for her make-up. She normally only ever used the lightest touch of foundation and blusher, but she was glad she'd bothered to bring it with her tonight—a glance in the mirror showed her that some repair work was needed!

Presently she began to calm down from the effects of the night's bombshell, and she sat for a moment on the pretty stool in the corner, pondering her next move where Maximus Seymour was concerned. She wished she could just press a button and make him disappear! She bit her lip so hard that it hurt as she thought about what had happened eight years ago. *Eight years!* Shouldn't she have allowed time to do its healing by now? she asked herself. She was well aware that she had inherited an over-sensitive disposition, but wasn't it time for some closure? That thought might once have been possible before tonight, she thought—but now the vital thing was to leave Farmhouse Cottage immediately, without raising any eyebrows.

Feeling more like herself, Candida walked towards the babble of voices coming from the end of the hall. As soon as she went into the room she could see Faith standing in a group, together with her husband and Max. The woman immediately beckoned to Candida to join them, raising her voice to make herself heard.

'Candida! Come over here!' she said, as she came towards them. 'Everyone is so impressed with it all— and *so* much of it is down to you!'

'Oh—well—I had a beautiful place to deal with,' Candida said. 'And I've enjoyed every single minute…it hasn't seemed like work at all!' For once, Candida thought privately, there'd been no difficult clients to convince!

Faith hooked her arm through Candida's. 'We *must* keep in touch, Candida! Promise me you will! I feel as if I've known you all my life—in fact you're one of the family now! I've been telling Maxy all about you! And Emily's always asking where Candy is!'

Candida smiled faintly, deliberately not looking at Max—who, she could sense, was gazing down at her. 'Oh, I'm sure we'll see each other now and then, Faith—' she began, but the woman interrupted.

'I'll make sure of it! If necessary I'll think of more work for you to do here!'

Candida didn't really take much notice of Faith's remarks—they were the sort of thing people said in the flush of the moment, she thought. But one thing was certain: somehow or other she would end her relationship with this family straight away. There was no way she'd risk being in Maximus Seymour's company ever again. The tangible affection they all showed each other meant that Max and his wife were regular visitors here, so she must cut herself off now, at this point, without hurting Faith's feelings. Looking at the woman, Candida felt a pang of regret at this decision. Faith would have been a lovely friend to have, she thought— someone to share things with, to confide in. How a sister and brother could be so different in personality was hard to understand. One so warm and kind, the other hard and unfeeling...and so full of self-importance! Ugh!

Then she remembered the way Max's warm hands had massaged her feet, had eased her toes, one by one, and she shuddered involuntarily. It would appear that the man *was* capable of gentleness...when he felt like it!

'You're not cold, are you, Candida?' Faith said, noting her tremble.

'No—no, of course not.' Candida hesitated. 'I really ought to be going, but I can't leave without a peep at Emily. Am I allowed?'

'Of course you are!' the woman said at once. 'Come on—you won't disturb her, because I'm happy to say she's reached the stage when she sleeps through anything!'

As they went up the stairs together, Faith said, touching Candida's arm for a second, 'I hope Max is behaving himself. Don't let his manner put you off, will you? I know he's got a reputation for having a difficult temperament sometimes—his work's the problem—but it's all a front, you know.'

Well, you *would* say that, Candida thought briefly.

'I know he's anxious about his next book,' Faith confided. 'It's due out next month. The critics weren't particularly kind about the last one, though sales weren't affected too much, I'm glad to say. But he doesn't take kindly to criticism, I'm afraid.'

Join the club! Candida thought. So… Faith obviously assured that she, Candida, knew who Max was. She must think that his name had cropped up in one of their conversations, or that she'd recognised his famous face. Candida shrugged inwardly. Well, she'd go along with that. There was no point in doing anything else.

Together they went into the child's bedroom, and Candida bent over the side of the cot, gently smoothing the tiny cheek with her finger.

'She's so adorable, Faith,' she whispered. 'You must be very proud of her.'

'Oh, of course… But life is never the same once you've got one of these! As you'll know yourself one day, Candida.'

'Perhaps,' Candida said slowly, thinking briefly again about Grant, and how charming and persuasive he'd been. He'd taken over her life in a way she'd never experienced before, allowing her to think in her private moments that he might one day be the father of her children. How wrong could you be?

After a minute or two, Rick put his head around the door. 'The Thompsons are about to leave, Faith,' he said quietly.

'Oh—OK.' She turned to Candida. 'I'll just go and

wish them goodnight—you come down when you're ready, Candida.'

'I'll only be another minute or two,' Candida said, still with her eyes on the sleeping child.

Standing in the pretty bedroom that smelt so sweetly of fragrant, warm baby, Candida felt her eyes prickle with unexpected tears. What little plans and expectations would Emily have for herself? she thought. How would life unfold for her? At this moment all she had to do was grow and flourish in the loving care of her parents, but one day she would have to face the world and sort out her own life.

A sudden movement behind her made Candida turn around quickly. Max came to stand at her side.

'Are you a member of the Emily Admiration Society too?' he asked quietly, and without waiting for her to answer, he said, 'Our first baby. Isn't she wonderful?'

Candida was genuinely surprised at his words. Who could imagine hard-nosed Maximus Seymour drooling over a baby? But it was obvious that he couldn't take his eyes off his little niece.

Neither of them spoke for a moment, then, without looking at her, he said quietly, 'Are you OK? I thought you looked very pale just now…almost as if you'd seen a ghost!'

Candida looked away, embarrassed at his words. But not really surprised. The man was a professional writer, with something of an awesome reputation for hard-hitting opinions. The study of human nature, with all its nuances, would be a permanent occupation for him, she thought, and a small chill ran through her. He could no doubt interpret and read people's actions and intentions as easily as reading a newspaper headline, but the thought didn't do anything to alter her opinion of him as self-serving and callous. Many of his books reflected this, she thought instinctively, even though she hadn't read any for a very, *very* long time!

'I'm feeling perfectly fine, thank you,' she lied. 'But I have been overdoing it on the work front lately—perhaps I'm due for a short holiday!' She shifted uncomfortably as she spoke. There was no need for him to stand quite so close to her, she thought. They were actually touching as they stood there together looking down at the baby, and she could feel the warmth of his body penetrating the fine silk of her dress. Why didn't he go around to the other side of the cot? She'd been there first!

Moving away from him decisively, she wondered if the time would ever come when she'd be able to cut him down to size! When she'd be able to give Mr Maximus Seymour a piece of her mind! She'd rehearsed the words silently many times, goodness only knew! Well, they were here now, together, breathing the same air. Why didn't she do it now—*now*? But a celebration party at his sister's house was not the right occasion, that was obvious. And anyway—what *would* she say to him after all this time? He probably wouldn't even remember what he'd said and done eight years ago—how ignominious would *that* be? If his mind was a complete blank about the whole episode! She stared at him unseeingly for a moment—maybe she'd never be able to do it, maybe all her vitriol must be locked away for ever, and she'd have to continue seething in private for the rest of her life!

Suddenly, a small gurgle from the cot made them both look down—to see Emily's huge blue eyes staring up at them. Without a second's hesitation, Max reached to pick her up, holding her close to him.

'Hello, Emmy,' he said softly. 'How's my little princess, then…um?'

The child folded her chubby arms around Max's neck and chuckled. 'Maxy—me come down now?'

'Oh, I don't think so, darling,' Max said, nuzzling his face into the small neck. 'Mummy might not like that.'

'Now, what's going on here, may I ask?' Faith said, coming into the room. 'Maxy, you just *cannot* be trusted, can you?' She smiled at Candida. 'I knew he'd have to have a cuddle before the night was out.' She smoothed Emily's arm. 'Did naughty Maxy wake you, Emily?' she said.

Emily gave a contented chuckle as she thrust her tiny fingers into Max's hair and gave it a tug. 'Me come down now, Mama?'

'Oh, go on, then,' Faith said. 'There are still some guests who'd like to see you, I'm sure.'

They all left the room, Max holding Emily closely in his arms as they went. Candida wondered what he was whispering into the child's ear, but whatever it was Emily was giggling happily, and she was forced to acknowledge that this was a very different human being from the one who had filled her imagination and her resentful thoughts for so long. She shook herself inwardly. What did it matter now, anyway? Permanent damage had been done and could never be undone.

Downstairs, they joined the small group of guests still remaining, and a general burst of delight greeted the baby's appearance. Emily seemed to know just what to do to make herself irresistible. Smiling and chuckling, she allowed herself to be passed happily from one to another.

'Just like a woman,' Max observed casually to Candida, as they stood together, watching. 'Feminine wiles must arrive with the package. She's only two, and just look how she's working the audience.'

Candida didn't make any reply to that, and was glad when Rick came over with a tray of drinks.

'Come on, you two,' he said breezily. 'We've got to finish another couple of bottles of this. Can't let them go to waste.'

Although glad of the diversion, Candida didn't really feel like any more alcohol. She'd already consumed more this evening than she'd normally drink in a month, she reminded herself. What she really felt like was a mug of hot, strong tea, but since that wasn't on offer she accepted the wine from Rick, smiling up at him.

'I ought to be on my way soon,' she said, realising that it was well after midnight—and certainly past her normal bedtime. She'd forgotten the pressures of being a party girl, and she was tired! She took a long drink, relishing the feel of the cold liquid in her mouth and throat—which she was aware had felt very dry all evening. She drained the glass and, looking up, realised that Max had been watching her, a cynical expression on his rugged features.

'That's called getting it down in one,' he said off-handedly.

Candida flushed at his words, suddenly feeling very hot, and looked away. 'I—I was—I mean, I'm very thirsty tonight, for some reason,' she said.

They stood there together for a few moments without saying any more, half listening to the CD which was playing softly in the corner.

Faith took Emily in her arms, glancing around her. 'I think it's time for one young lady to go back to bed,' she said, and the remaining guests made final moves to go as well. They bade everyone goodnight, as Rick showed them out, and soon Max and Candida were the only ones left in the room.

'I really must be on my way as well,' Candida said quickly. 'I'm not used to all this celebrating, and—'

Suddenly, and without warning, she felt her knees weaken, and she leaned against the side of an armchair to steady herself. Immediately she felt Max's strong hand under her elbow, then encircling her waist, as her legs finally refused to support her, and gave way. She leaned into him helplessly as he lowered her gently into the depths of a comfy seat.

'Stay there for a bit,' he said. 'I'll fetch you some water.'

In a minute or two he returned, and Candida took the glass from him, drinking shakily. That was better, she thought. Or…was it? Because now the room was starting to spin—ever so slowly at first, then more rapidly, like a rollercoaster warming up towards its dizzying performance. Starting to panic, Candida pulled herself forward until, totally unable to do anything about it, she began to slide gracefully from the chair onto the floor, the only thing audible to her being the loud drumming of her heart in her ears.

She learned afterwards that she was out for several minutes, and when she did come round it was to find herself stretched out on one of the sofas, with a cold cloth on her forehead and Max kneeling beside her, rubbing her hands briskly between his, repeating her name, over and over again, with his face so close to hers that she could feel his breath on her cheeks. She struggled desperately to raise herself into a sitting position, but he immediately eased her back down, his hands firmly on her shoulders.

'Stay still,' he ordered. 'This will pass in a minute. You're finally returning to earth.'

'I'm fine now...really...' she said weakly. 'Oh, dear...what a party-pooper! It's all the wine—and I've been fighting a chill for several days...'

Taking stock of her situation, Candida realised that she should never have come here tonight. She'd known that. Her body had been warning her since Wednesday, when she'd woken up with a slight temperature and a sore throat. But she'd managed to convince herself that it was nothing, and she'd fought it off—because, like a child, she'd been looking forward to going to a party. To a Saturday night out. And especially to coming to Farmhouse Cottage.

'If you think you're going home or going anywhere tonight, you can think again,' Max said dismissively. 'For one thing, you're not fit to be behind the wheel of a car—you must be well over the limit.' He paused. 'You hardly ate anything at supper, did you, Candida? You've only had a few drinks, but on a practically empty stomach. I concluded that you were either on a strict diet—though why, I couldn't imagine—or that you weren't feeling well.'

Oh, dear, Candida thought. She had tried to disguise the fact that she'd helped herself to very little food by spreading it around on her plate a bit…but obviously it hadn't escaped the observations of *Sir*!

'I am very grateful for your concern, Max,' she began, 'but—'

'There are no buts,' he interrupted. 'You can go home tomorrow. A good night's sleep will work wonders—there are plenty of bedrooms here, as you know very well.'

This suggestion—or command!—made Candida feel even worse. She couldn't possibly stay here—she hadn't brought an overnight bag or anything with her!

'That's not going to happen,' she said, trying to inject an authoritative note into her voice. 'I am going *home*!'

Max sat back on his heels and shook his head slowly. Gazing across at him, Candida was painfully, hatefully aware of his achingly handsome face, of those blue-black eyes that could express a hint of menace one minute and an irrefutably desirable manly warmth the next.

'I can see that I am going to have to exert some physical pressure to make you see sense,' he said, standing up. 'I thought a few minutes ago that I was going to have to give you the kiss of life, but…' He paused, a maddening glint appearing in his eyes. 'Sadly for me, you came to just in time.'

Candida stared at him unbelievingly. Was the man making a *pass* at her? she thought, not wanting to think it. Didn't he have *any* conscience? He was married— and she was a guest in his sister's house. It was hardly the right kind of behaviour—especially from a man of his standing! It did nothing to alter her opinion of him— far from it—and only doubled her antagonism. Even if she *was* honest enough to confess that she found him physically attractive. Perish *that* thought. *Now!*

Candida sat up properly then, but realised as soon as she did so that Max was probably right about her not being able to go home tonight. She was feeling distinctly woozy and distant, and was actually longing to lie down and go to sleep. 'Well,' she said shakily, 'we'll have to see what Faith says….'

'My sister will be delighted that you're staying the night,' he said at once. 'Her hospitable nature is well known. And,' he added, 'I *always* stay over, because Sunday lunch in this household is a very indulgent tradition.' He paused. 'By then you may feel able to eat something, so that by tomorrow afternoon you'll be fit to go home.'

So, Candida thought helplessly, he was planning her life out for her, and it seemed there was nothing she could do about it.

Just then Faith and Rick came back in, and Max told his sister about his suggestion that Candida should stay the night—she was grateful that he omitted to mention the fact that she'd fainted.

Faith clapped her hands delightedly. 'Of *course* you must stay, Candida—we'd love that, wouldn't we, Rick?'

'It'd be great to have you here, Candida,' Rick said at once.

'I just love the rooms being used,' Faith went on. 'You can have the blue room—with Max to one side, and Emily on the other. And—'

'And *we'll* have a bit of peace, because one of you will have the pleasure of Emily's wake-up call,' Rick said, smiling. 'She's very bright first thing. And for once our ears will be closed.'

'I can let you have anything you'll need for the night, Candida,' Faith said, 'and something to replace that wonderful dress for tomorrow.' She looked around, smiling happily. 'And,' she said, her enthusiasm for the plan gaining momentum, 'I've bought a splendid leg of lamb from the farm down the road—their meat is always wonderful. So, there you are—everyone get up for breakfast whenever you feel like it, and we'll all have a lovely leisurely lunch later.'

Much as Candida liked the way she was being made to feel so welcome, so wanted here, she couldn't help feeling distinctly helpless—and uneasy. Her next twenty-four hours were being completely taken out of her hands, and she was being drawn into a cosy family gathering which included the man she had no time for. It was beginning to do her head in! If only the lovely Ella had agreed to come tonight, she thought. Max wouldn't have been giving her all this attention, and it would have been easier to make a quick departure in the morning. Instead of which, a party to celebrate the completion of her work was turning into a long weekend in which *she* was having to make up a foursome with someone she'd often dreamed of strangling!

Later, in the blue room she'd been allocated, Candida undressed and showered, before slipping into the rather short T-shirt nightdress which Faith had lent her. It ended well above her knees, but would be comfortable enough, she thought. She released her hair from its knot, thinking briefly that it was time she had it trimmed—it fell below her shoulders, and always took ages to dry after shampooing. Then, with a thankful sigh, she crawled under the duvet, switched off the bedside lamp, and closed her eyes. But would she *ever* be able to sleep? she asked herself. The thought that two doors away Max Seymour was also to spend the night filled her with such a mix of emotions she felt like screaming!

In spite of everything Candida eventually felt herself slipping into a half-doze, silly dreams popping in and out of her mind, when suddenly a quiet tap on the door brought her back to full consciousness. She sat up immediately, got out of bed, and padded across the room. Faith had obviously thought of something she might need, she thought—the woman's generosity and kindness were overwhelming.

She threw the door open wide. But it wasn't Faith. It was Max standing there, still fully dressed. He leant casually against the doorframe, his gaze fixed on Candida's appearance…on her long, slender legs beneath the inadequate nightdress, its round neckline and loose fabric clearly exhibiting her pretty figure, and the long, tumbling waves of hair framing her face—a face devoid, now, of any makeup. A rosy blush began to slowly creep up from her neck as she stood there, waiting for some explanation as to why he'd disturbed her.

'Hmm,' he began laconically, 'I don't know which dress I prefer you in…'

'Is there something the matter?' Candida asked, unable to keep the trace of hostility she was feeling from showing—a hostility born of the fact that she felt so unutterably useless standing there with practically nothing on.

'Nope,' he said, unconcerned. 'I didn't feel like going to bed yet, so I went downstairs for a glass of water and happened to see this in the corner of the sofa…' He put his hand in his pocket and lazily pulled out her clutch bag. 'I thought you might need it,' he added.

She didn't take it immediately, but stared at him for a long moment. Did he *really* think she'd fall for that one? she asked herself. It went back to Victorian melodrama, with the lady mislaying her perfect white glove! Much as Candida's experience with the male sex was fairly limited, she knew opportunism when she saw it! He was obviously hoping that he'd be invited inside. One-night stands would be a common enough practice for someone like him…and the fact that he had a wife would be neither here nor there. Just a bit of fun, no harm done—and anyway he and Ella seemed perfectly happy to go their separate ways from time to time. Well, if he thought *she* was going to fall in with his lustful ambitions, he was going to be unlucky!

She reached forward and took her bag from him with a faint smile of acknowledgement. She must remember that they were both guests here. She must try and at least be gracious to the man. 'Oh, thanks,' she said. 'You shouldn't have bothered…it could have waited until morning.'

'It was no bother,' he drawled, looking as fresh and wide-awake as ever, and making no effort to go. He was an incredibly tall man, she thought again—or perhaps the fact that she was standing there in her bare feet made him seem more so.

'I also wondered if…if you were feeling OK now,' he went on. 'You haven't had a recurrence of whatever it was you had earlier, I hope?'

'No. Thank you,' she said firmly. 'Your administrations seemed to have worked perfectly well. There's no need for you to be concerned on my behalf.'

He didn't reply to that, but stood there, just staring at her.

'Well, goodnight, then,' she said decisively. 'I hope the glass of water helps you get to sleep—eventually.'

He merely nodded his own goodnight as she turned and went back inside, closing the door firmly.

She waited silently on the other side, listening for his departing footsteps, but he made no sound at all, and after several moments Candida had the greatest difficulty in not peeping outside to see if he'd gone. Then, shrugging, she went back to bed, pulling the duvet up around her shoulders.

By now all thoughts of rest seemed to have deserted her, and she lay tossing and turning for ages. Blast the man, she thought. Before his intrusion she'd almost managed to drift off, but now she felt as if she could get up and do a day's work with no problem!

Cross with herself, she turned over for the hundredth time, forcing her eyes shut, then opened them again, staring over to the window, where the beautiful heavy drapes hung luxuriously…drapes which *she* had selected, along with almost everything else in this room. She would never have imagined that one day she'd be sleeping—or trying to sleep—in a client's house. Nor that she would find herself in the position she now was—wishing that Maximus Seymour was lying beside her, with his warm, sensitive hands on her body, his handsome face close to hers.

She sighed, deeply irritated at the thoughts which refused to leave her. Was it possible, she asked herself bleakly, to fancy someone you actually thought you loathed? She'd heard all about the 'appeal of the rotter'—how some women couldn't resist a man who'd actually physically abused them. Was this what was happening to her now?

Then she sat up, mentally pulling herself together. Face the problem and deal with it, she commanded herself! This time tomorrow she'd be safely tucked up in her own bed—with all the events of this particular evening already beginning to fade from her mind.

CHAPTER THREE

AT TWO-THIRTY the following Tuesday, Candida paused for a second outside the apartment on the top floor of the imposing Thameside building, glancing at the slip of paper in her hand to make sure she'd come to the right address. And *what* an address! She'd never set foot in such a place before in her life! The female client who'd spoken to her on the telephone to make the arrangement had seemed very precise and authoritative, with a rather forbidding attitude, Candida had thought at the time. But she was used to dealing with awkward customers. If she could get this one to be amenable to her suggestions it could be a lucrative contract. Fingers crossed, she thought, as she rang the bell.

After a few moments, the door opened, and standing there in front of her—seeming to use up all the space between them—was Max Seymour, almost blocking out the light. Candida's mouth dropped open in total disbelief and surprise. She was unable to find her voice to say a single word. What on earth was *he* doing here? she thought wildly.

'Ah—Candida—' he said pleasantly, standing

aside and sweeping his arm in an expansive gesture to invite her in.

'But…um…how…?' She stared down again at the paper with the name she'd been given. 'I thought Mr John Dean lived here—' she began, and he interrupted at once.

'Quite right—he does. Do come in.'

Still mystified, Candida allowed him to usher her inside, then turned to look at him.

He was dressed casually, as before, but today his black cotton shirt was open at the neck to reveal tanned skin and a strong growth of body hair. His light-coloured chinos seemed to emphasise the length of his legs, and as he moved he reminded Candida of a panther…sleek, elegant and mysterious—which she'd been all too conscious of at the party!

He looked down at her quizzically. 'Allow me to explain,' he said, without preamble. 'John Dean is my "aka"—which Janet, my secretary, always uses on my behalf with strangers, or when making casual appointments. Having a…shall we say well-known name can work against one from time to time.' He paused. 'It's a very useful ploy,' he added. 'It means I always have the advantage.'

Oh, yes, of course, Candida thought bitterly. That's just like you. You obviously need to be the one pulling all the strings. She forced herself to appear calm and unruffled, which was difficult because she was feeling exactly the opposite. She swallowed, and when she spoke her voice was cool.

'Why couldn't you have told me at the weekend that I'd be coming to see you?' she said. 'It would have been a—friendly, not to say mannerly thing to do.'

'It completely slipped my mind,' he said cheerfully, and Candida thought, Well, that's a total lie! It obviously amused him to tease her!

'And Faith didn't mention it either.'

'No, because I didn't bother to tell her,' he said coolly. If he *had*, he thought briefly, his sister would have given him a strong lecture about how to deal with this particular young woman, and warned him not to treat her in the way he sometimes did members of the opposite sex.

'Anyway,' he went on, 'does it matter? You're here now. Have a look around and see what you can suggest to improve my working conditions.'

Determined to be business-like, Candida looked around her, overwhelmed by the opulence of the place and wondering what *she* could do to improve it. She was also thinking that it was a good thing she'd had no idea who she was coming to see today, because there was no way she'd have allowed herself to be involved with this man. She wasn't that hard up for business!

The whole feel of this room was an overpoweringly masculine one—lined as it was with heavily laden bookshelves, and not a tidy corner anywhere to be seen. Totally different from Farmhouse Cottage and its warm, intimate atmosphere, which Max had said he envied. Though of course, Candida thought, it would be his wife who preferred *this* location—close to shops and theatres and humming London life—even though she apparently needed to escape at the weekend.

He looked down at her thoughtfully, and she knew instinctively that he was doing his own assessing—of her. And taking in every detail of her appearance. She was wearing well-cut jeans and loose cream cashmere sweater, with a flimsy multi-coloured scarf tied loosely at the neck, her hair tied back in a ponytail.

'May I offer you tea?' he asked suddenly. 'I can't run to cucumber sandwiches, but I've bought some cakes from the deli across the road…'

Candida looked up at him. 'I'd like a cup of tea,' she said, almost reluctantly, because she was still feeling as if she'd like to pour one over his head! 'No sugar, thanks.'

He turned away. 'You're wearing different perfume,' he said casually. 'It's very…"you", shall we say?'

Candida stared at his retreating back, but made no comment as he went towards what was obviously the kitchen. She realised that he was very perceptive, and, yes, it was true she did use a lighter floral scent for daytime—but his worming his way into her life was un-nerving. It was something Grant had also managed to do, with apparently no effort at all. It must be her fault, she thought.

'Make yourself at home,' he said. 'I'll show you around in a minute.'

Candida walked slowly over to the huge windows that overlooked the Thames, and held her breath for a second. It was a spectacular view of the river in both di-rections, from Westminster to St Paul's and across to the London Eye. She glanced around her pensively. So this was where all the creative forces were at work—this was where inspiration flowed! A strange chill ran through her as she imagined the man, either at his computer, or with a pad on his knee, frowning in concentration. Was this, perhaps, this very spot where he'd taken up a pen and put a black line through her dreams?

Candida felt a kind of morbid fascination sweep over her as she went slowly through the apartment, peering into each room. Here was his study, with the usual paraphernalia—stacks of writing materials, dictionaries, reference books, and a long shelf containing, it would seem, all his own titles. She recognised the ones she'd read and, moving across, ran her finger along the leather-bound edges. *A Certain Dilemma...Marking the Torrent...Listing to Starboard*—and many more she'd never set eyes on. His stories were always strong, philosophical, some of the prose hardened by cruelty—direct or indirect.

Candida shivered involuntarily, still not quite believing that she was actually this close to the man after all this time. It was hard to relate the author to the person she'd spent much of the weekend with, and in whose company she was about to take afternoon tea! She hoped her guardian angel hadn't gone off duty—she had the feeling that she was going to need all the help she could get!

As so often happened when she was living inside her own mind, Candida was unaware of things going on around her, and his voice suddenly interrupting her thoughts made her jump. She felt her cheeks go crimson, as if she'd been caught red-handed at something illegal!

'D'you like reading?' he asked peremptorily.

'Yes. I'm miserable if I haven't got at least one good book on the go,' she replied, not looking up at him.

His lip curled slightly, and he nodded at the books on the shelf. 'Have you read any of mine?'

'I've read *Marking the Torrent* and *Listing to*

Starboard—and a couple of others I can't quite remember at the moment,' she said airily.

'I have difficulty remembering some of them myself.' He looked down at her. 'What did you think of the ones you *have* read? Did you *enjoy* them?'

Candida stared at him for a moment. The way he put the question didn't feel as if he was fishing for compliments—it seemed a genuine enquiry, as if he really needed to know what she thought of his writing. She drew in her breath for a second. Was this the moment to say that his books were not for her, that she found the prose 'flat and dull, albeit with moments of surprising delicacy and warmth'…or that the dialogue was 'often strained and sometimes pointless'…and he should perhaps 'go away and think hard before returning pen to paper'? The words he had used to describe *her* first and only novel eight years earlier! To see that criticism in a national newspaper had caused her so much anguish and hurt that the raw pain in her heart seemed indelible, and her embarrassment was still as acute as ever.

But Candida could not, in all honesty, say any of that—because Maximus Seymour was a master of his art, and even if one of his epics didn't receive the normal acclaim, it was always still a work of consummate skill in the craft of writing. Sales of his books proved the point only too well.

'I don't always enjoy *some* of a book,' she said slowly, in answer to his question, 'and sometimes what you write disturbs me. I find myself wondering why you allowed a certain character to behave in the way he or she did. As I read, I sometimes anticipate at least three other scenarios than the one *you* chose, and—'

'That's good! Great!' Max said. 'My books do not feature foregone conclusions because life is not like that, and—'

'Yes, but neither is life so often as dark and uneasy as you portray it,' Candida countered. 'For most of us, anyway.'

'I write fiction, remember,' he said, a sudden coldness in his tone.

'I'm well aware of that. But even fiction needs to relate to what will *probably* happen to people,' Candida said. 'I find some of your twists and turns unbelievable— and I need to *believe* in what the protagonists are up to! Suspending disbelief has its limits, surely? And,' she added hotly, 'you can be unnecessarily cruel—as if you *enjoy* the hurt! I can feel you wallowing in it at times!'

They were facing each other now, a bit like two sparring partners in a ring, and Max was aware of the pretty flush that had coloured Candida's features. He liked a woman with opinions she wasn't afraid to express, he thought, and this one fell into *that* category in spades— despite her general naivety, which had been transparent as soon as they'd met. The only person who ever faulted his work was his editor—everyone else, all his friends and associates, and especially Faith and the family, always thought that his work was beyond any criticism at all! And now here was this woman, whom he was towering above in the confines of his study, having a go at him….sticking pins in his delicate sensitivities! And for some reason he was enjoying the experience!

'And in *The Final Beginning*,' Candida went on, unable to stop herself now that she'd started, 'I don't know why you killed off Theodore… It really upset me at the time.'

'Why? What else should I have done with him?' Max said, almost sulkily.

'Oh, well… Think of Rochester in *Jane Eyre*—you could have *blinded* Theodore, made him really dependent on Alexandra at last. That way they would have had time for each other, to live together, to—to…love each other. Because they did love each other, didn't they? You made us believe that!' She swallowed, shaking her head quickly. 'It was terrible to cut them off from each other at that point. Heartless!'

Staring up at him, her eyes misting with emotion at what she'd just been saying, she was surprised at the expression on Max's face. He was looking at her closely, his brows drawn together slightly, a nerve twitching noticeably in his neck. Candida caught her breath for a moment. She'd gone too far—really upset him now, she thought. Well, *good*!

But suddenly he pursed his lips dismissively and smiled down at her. 'Well,' he said, 'thanks for your input, Candida. Maybe I'll get you to proof-read for me some time. Point out where I'm going wrong.'

Now she really did blush, but she was determined not to back down. 'You did ask what I thought,' she said coolly.

'Exactly. It's useful to hear a reader's opinion— bearing in mind that all opinions are subjective. There's no way any writer can please everyone all the time.'

Somehow it seemed to Candida that they were more on a level footing now. Even though she hadn't yet had the guts to embarrass him—if he was capable of being embarrassed about *anything*—by informing him of how he'd killed off her ambitions for ever. But she'd keep that for another time—save it up! Because, in spite of not knowing how or when she was going to do it, she realised again that she wouldn't rest until it was finally out of her system. For good. In the meantime, she felt that she'd ruffled his literary feathers—just for a few seconds—by speaking her mind. And the look on his face supported his sister's remarks that he didn't take kindly to criticism from *anyone*! In a funny sort of way, Candida felt that they were at the 'one all' stage!

He had set the tea things on a small table by the window, and they sat down together on a squashy black low leather sofa. Leaning forward, he poured tea from a stainless steel teapot into two mugs, then handed her one, offering her a plate of delicious-looking Danish pastries.

'My favourites,' Candida said, taking one and placing it on the small paper napkin he'd given her.

'I seldom eat much during the day,' he said. 'The trouble with working at home means that it would be so easy to over-indulge—keep raiding the fridge. So I've made it a rule to stick to black coffee most of the time. Keeps me alert, and reasonably imaginative—even if my writing doesn't always come up to standard in some people's eyes,' he added sarcastically.

Candida took a bite from her pastry, and refused to feel awkward any more about what she'd said. After all, she'd *paid* for his books—and they were always in the top price bracket—and he had *asked* for her opinion. That was what he'd got!

Max watched her nibble at the cake, thinking that this was a really rather exceptional woman. Not only beautiful—his sister always contrived to sit him next to beautiful women at her parties—but intelligent, and with a clear mind of her own. He liked that, and felt strangely complimented at the way she'd talked about his books—how she'd entered into the ones she'd read, got into the minds of his characters and what happened to them. He sensed at once that she was deeply imaginative…a kindred spirit in some ways, he thought. A slow smile crossed his elegant features. Maybe he could have a bit of fun with Ms Candida Greenway!

Presently he took Candida on a tour of the flat. As she had already observed, most of it was in immaculate condition. The only things which could do with replacing were the drapes and the floor coverings—though privately Candida thought there wasn't that much wrong with the existing ones.

Eventually, standing together by the window, they watched the scene below—even more beautiful now, as the sun was beginning to sink—and Candida felt a pang of envy. Her poor little flat couldn't compare with any of this, she thought. It would be idyllic to live in a place like this.

Just then, Max's mobile rang. He turned away to answer it while Candida wandered into the main bedroom, with its king-size bed covered by a hastily thrown duvet. She could hear him speaking on the phone, then he came in to stand beside her.

'That's a pain,' he said. 'I'm afraid I've got to go and fetch Ella home now. Sorry to bring our meeting to such an early close.'

'Oh, that's OK' Candida said easily, thinking, good, she could go home!

He glanced at his watch. 'D'you feel like coming with me?' he asked suddenly. 'Ella's been staying with friends of ours in the country…it takes about an hour from here, and I hate travelling alone.' He paused. 'Besides—I want to hear some more of your valuable opinions.'

Candida was staggered at the suggestion, and was about to decline with an excuse—any excuse—when he went on.

'Look, it's nearly four o'clock. If we go now we'll be there just after five, and it's a super run once we get clear of town. When we come back it'll be getting dark, and then we could have a bit of supper somewhere before dropping you back home.'

'Oh, I don't really think—' Candida began, but he interrupted.

'What's the problem? he said. 'I realise you didn't bring your own car here today, so the least I can do is see you safely back to your place later. You'll be doing me a favour,' he added quickly, before Candida could pour cold water on his suggestion. 'I prefer to have someone in the passenger seat. Consider it part of the commission,' he added. 'Put it on the bill.'

Candida looked at him helplessly. He had made it virtually impossible to refuse without sounding stand-offish and negative. Anyway, she had nothing else to do, and it *was* a gorgeous September afternoon. It might be quite pleasant.

'Jack and Daisy—our friends—are apparently having to go to Brussels on business a day earlier than they thought,' he said. 'So Ella needs to come home today, rather than tomorrow, which was the original plan.'

'Oh, well, then…all right—if it would really suit you for me to go with you,' Candida said hesitantly.

'It would suit me very well, thanks. So that's settled.' Max grinned down at Candida, and the girl's heart missed a beat. He was an outstandingly handsome man, she thought again, not wanting to think it—or rather, not wanting to think that she cared one way or the other. But it was difficult—what normal woman disliked being in the company of one of nature's favourites?

Presently they went downstairs to the lift, and made their way to the rear of the building, where all the owners' cars were garaged. As she might have expected, Max's was a sleek silver Mercedes, and he handed her in to the passenger side. Sinking into the enveloping leather seat, Candida let out a little sigh, thinking about her own ten year old banger of a car and the bill she'd just paid for two new tyres. She wondered what two new tyres for *this* would cost!

Painfully conscious of Max's overt masculinity, of the thrust of his jaw as he looked to left and right as they went towards the motorway, Candida wondered whether in a minute she was going to wake up from all this. She had never dreamed that she would ever really meet this man—let alone be this close! In two or three days life had unwrapped several unbelievable layers of incidents and coincidences to bring her to this point. Sitting so close to him, she felt distinctly vulnerable, with thoughts that disturbed her. The occasional lazy movement of his strong thighs beneath the fabric of his trousers *would* keep sending ripples of sexual excitement through her, and for an unbelievable moment Candida felt that her principles could easily be persuaded to desert her! She forced her gaze away quickly, shocked by those brief seconds of lustful intensity that had taken her unawares.

He was right about the journey. Once they'd left the motorway the countryside looked wonderful in the mellow sunshine, and Candida found herself enjoying the experience of being somewhere different, *with* someone different. Someone *very* different!

Max glanced across at her. 'You haven't gone to sleep on me, have you?' he asked softly, and she blushed, realising that they hadn't spoken for several miles. The fact was that being in this luxurious car was like being wafted along on a summer breeze, and the silence between them suggested something of a companionable atmosphere, she thought, surprised at how quickly she had relaxed.

She cleared her throat and looked across at him. 'Your…Ella…Ella obviously doesn't drive?' she asked, thinking, What a daft question to ask—of *course* the woman didn't drive, or she wouldn't need to be collected!

He shot a glance at her, a slow smile touching his lips, then turned back to stare ahead. 'No, no, I'm afraid Ella doesn't drive,' he said. 'I'm convinced she'd never get through a test. Probably something to do with her nerves.' He paused. 'I must say, it would have been useful at times if she did, but there you go.'

Just after five, they turned off the road onto an unmade track leading down towards a valley, with fields on either side rolling away gently as they drove slowly along. From the top of the hill some farm buildings were clearly visible.

Presently, Max pulled up beside a large farmhouse, and almost immediately a stocky young man came outside to greet them. Max introduced them.

'Candida—this is Jack, who's been entertaining Ella for me for a few days, and Jack—Candida is an interior designer who's going to be sorting things out at the apartment.'

'Hi, Candida,' Jack said easily. 'Sorry you won't see my wife, but she's had to pop up to the shop for a few last-minute things.'

'Where's Ella?' Max asked.

'Where she always is at this time of the day…lying down on the bed!' Jack grinned.

They all went inside, and he called up the stairs. 'Ella—Ella—wake up! Maxy's here!'

Suddenly, hurtling down the stairs and racing into the room, a large black Labrador appeared, and jumped straight into Max's arms, covering him with sloppy kisses. Max grabbed the dog's head to one side and looked across at Candida, whose expression said it all—most of it unrepeatable! The impossible brute—how *could* he? she thought! He'd deliberately allowed her to think that Ella was his wife! He obviously found it a constant source of amusement to put her at a disadvantage. To make her look as small as she felt.

For a few moments words just wouldn't materialize for Candida, but slowly her hand went up to her mouth. She didn't want to see the joke—but Max felt no such constraints, and his deep chuckle rumbled around the room as he looked across at her

'Is this a private joke?' Jack asked mildly, looking at each of them in turn.

'Yes—sorry, Jack, I'm afraid it is. We'll tell you another time,' Max said, pushing the dog down and going towards the door. 'Thanks so much for giving Ella a break from the city life—she appreciates it, and so do I. But we'll set off now, because you're in a hurry to go—aren't you?'

'Yes—sorry about that. But at least let me offer you a drink?' Jack said.

'No—can't stop,' Max said, giving Candida a sidelong glance. 'Candida and I have got a dinner date tonight. Business to discuss,' he added.

Outside, the dog immediately jumped into the back of the car and sat bolt upright on her hindquarters, clearly happy to be back where she belonged.

As Max and Candida got in, they both turned inward to look at the dog, who was staring stolidly ahead between the two front seats.

'Meet the wi—' Max began, his eyes still glistening with mirth.

Candida interrupted him. 'Please shut up,' she said pleasantly. *'Just shut up!'*

CHAPTER FOUR

FOR the next few minutes Candida stared ahead of her as they began the return journey. Then, 'You might have *said* something,' she muttered.

'What about?' Max asked innocently, barely able to stop himself from laughing.

'You know very well what about. That we were going to collect a dog—not a wife!'

'What—and spoil the fun? Sorry, but I can't resist a joke…'

'As long as it's at someone else's expense!' Candida retorted.

'No—honestly, Candida, I had no idea that you thought I was married. When you made that remark about Ella not being able to drive, I couldn't resist perpetuating the misunderstanding.' He reached out a hand to touch her. Candida shifted her knee quickly.

'Well, if you ever do have a wife, I sincerely hope that she shares your sense of humour,' Candida said flatly.

'Oh, that's not likely…having a wife, I mean,' Max said at once. 'Writers do not make good partners—they're far too obsessive and *self*-obsessed, I'm afraid.' He paused, waiting to accelerate away as they rejoined the motorway. 'I don't give literary marriages much of a chance—even though my sister is constantly on the look-out for a suitable woman to share my bed. On a permanent basis, that is,' he added mischievously. 'She thinks all partnerships should be like hers. She and Rick were always meant for each other, and now with little Emmy...' He trailed off.

Glancing at him covertly, Candida was surprised at the softening expression on his features. What a strange mixture he was, she thought. As hard as a nut, but with something of a soft centre! Whatever he said about not wanting a wife, he certainly seemed to envy a family life. She frowned as her thoughts raced on, and she turned to look at him.

'I still think that you might have mentioned on Saturday that I would be coming to see *you* today,' she said. 'It was...underhand of you to keep me in the dark—whatever you say about "forgetting all about it".'

He raised his hand in a gesture of submission. 'I've obviously annoyed you, Candida, and for that I apologise,' he said, turning to face her for a second. 'But there's been no harm done, has there? No bones broken, so to speak?'

He returned his attention to the road, and the slight twitching at the corner of his mouth left Candida in no doubt that he considered the events of the whole afternoon a huge joke. Perhaps there were more surprises to come, she thought, irritated all over again. Why was it that people—men—seemed able to manipulate her to suit themselves?

As they made the journey back to town, with the dog snoring loudly on the seat behind them,

Candida's thoughts were in turmoil. She felt as if she was being whirled around in a spin dryer! Made to look stupid and uncertain of herself, being wrong-footed again, by the man sitting so smugly beside her. To her way of thinking he'd got her to his apartment under false pretences—how on earth was *she* to have known that he used another name? And then, worst of all, allowing her to think that they were to collect his wife... Now they were apparently returning to the apartment, to leave the dog with the housekeeper and her husband, who occupied a small flat at the front of the building.

Suddenly there was a stirring in the back seat, and Ella's head appeared, followed by her wet nose being rested on Candida's shoulder, and one large brown eye staring at her pensively. In spite of everything, Candida couldn't help smiling as she turned to smooth the dog's glossy head.

Max turned towards her briefly. 'Ah, Ella approves of you,' he said. 'That's quite unusual for her, on so short an acquaintance. She's very fussy who she befriends.'

'Then we share that much in common,' Candida said at once.

'Quite right too,' Max said. 'But seriously—the dog can be quite off-hand with people until she gets to know them. You must have something special about you, Candida.'

Candida shrugged, her natural good nature beginning to take over. 'We always had dogs at home,' she said. 'My father has a rather ancient Jack Russell—Toby— and I'd love to have one, but it just isn't practicable. I'm out working much of the time, and the clients I visit wouldn't value me bringing a dog with me. I couldn't bear to leave an animal for long stretches in the car by itself. It doesn't seem a fair way to treat them.'

Max nodded his agreement. 'When I'm writing Ella sits at my feet, and when I have to be away the Jarretts downstairs do the honours—take her to the park several times a day, even let her sleep at the foot of their bed at night. And of course Jack and Daisy give her a little holiday every now and then. They love having her down there. While the London parks are wonderful, there's nothing like the broad expanse of country fields for a dog—any dog—to roam, to feel free.' He paused, before adding, 'She's lucky, and so am I…it clears my conscience. Dogs need to be with people. They don't like being alone for long.'

Well, that was one point in his favour, Candida thought. He did consider his animal's welfare, and he obviously loved Ella…which proved that he wasn't quite as selfish as she'd thought. And, by his own admission earlier, he, too, liked company other than his own—which was why she'd been more or less forced into this afternoon's arrangements. Just because he said he liked to have someone sitting next to him in the car, she'd gone along with it like a lamb to the slaughter!

Her whole association with Max Seymour seemed to be taking on a surreal quality, she thought to herself as they drove—at what seemed to her enormous speed along the motorway. And the curious thing was that she had never even been properly introduced to the man It had obviously been assumed by Faith—and Rick—that she already knew the person she'd been sat next to at the party, or that he was so famous she *must* know him She had been carried along by a slipstream of events over which she'd had little control, and the realisation made her feel uneasy and out of her depth.

By the time they got back to the apartment, Candida had accepted the situation more or less gracefully. The work that was apparently expected of her was straight-forward enough. Merely to suggest suitable fabric for the drapes, and to recommend new alternatives for the floor coverings. The suppliers she used only stocked top-of-the-range products, and it wouldn't come cheap—but did *she* care? Max Seymour was obviously very wealthy—she'd bring him all the top-quality samples and swatches to choose from. He probably wouldn't even bother to ask about prices, she thought.

She glanced across at him as he concentrated on the road ahead. There was one good thing about all this, Candida thought—at least there was no picky wife to contend with! Someone who'd argue and disagree with every suggestion. He'll probably agree with everything I put forward, she thought. He would see the tiresome business of anything domestic as a hindrance to the most important thing in his life—his famous career, and being left in peace to continue doing it.

Candida's shoulders drooped for a second. Although she enjoyed the work she did, she, too, would love to be free to sit down and write—to really succeed this time. But having to stand on her own two feet and earn her living seemed to preclude that possibility. Writing was a serious business, she was well aware of that, demanding of time and commitment, and—annoyingly—fate had allowed *him* both those opportunities. Another brief feeling of envy swept over her as she thought of how cosseted Max must have been when starting out, with his mother aiding and abetting him all the way. She would have given him all the help and advice he could possibly have needed, to say nothing of introducing him to all the right people. It simply wasn't fair!

Max parked the car in his allotted space and Ella jumped out, standing obediently by his side as he helped Candida from the passenger seat. Then they all went together to the top floor, the dog bounding about happily.

'I'll just give Ella her supper, then we'll think about ours,' Max said, glancing at Candida. 'D'you want to freshen up? You know where everything is.'

Candida went into the spacious, well-appointed bathroom, and glanced in the glass at her appearance. Well, she'd somehow survived the occasion, she thought. Survived the unexpectedness of the afternoon's events.

But now she had the immediate prospect of being sociable with Max, who seemed to be playing with her like a cat playing with a mouse. He seemed to wear his own sense of superiority with a smugness which thoroughly irritated her, she thought. Then she shrugged. The atmosphere between them was suitably relaxed—apart from the small spat earlier about her opinion of his books. And why not? He had no idea of how she felt towards him—how could he have? He was in total ignorance of how he'd affected her life when she was so young and inexperienced. But it would be useless to deny that she found him attractive. He was famous, mature...and Faith's adored brother. That last fact alone shot him up the scale somewhat, Candida thought. Because Faith was the kindest, warmest person she had ever met. How could she and Max possibly be related? But they were, and it had to be a definite point in his

favour. And anyway—turning her thoughts to the immediate present—she was now starving! She'd had no
breakfast that day, and just an apple and some cheese
for lunch, and Max's teatime pastry to sustain her. Yes,
she thought, she'd agree to a decent meal in a nice restaurant without her arm being twisted!

She emerged from the bathroom, and Max glanced
at her as she came towards him. Faith had been more
than accurate, he thought, in her description of the girl.
Her casual, yet immaculate mode of dress appealed to
him—her shining hair, small feet and hands with well-
kept, unpolished nails, giving her an allure which extravagant clothes and make-up would be hard to equal.
And she always *smelled* wonderful, he mused. Not just
her choice of perfume, but her obvious overall fastidi-
ousness that reminded him of the pureness of an early
spring morning.

Hang on! he told himself. You're thinking of her like
a character in one of your books! This was no fictional
female, and she had plenty about her that told him she'd
be no push-over in any circumstances. He freely
admitted that he'd fancied her at his sister's party—
fancied her enough to go up to her room later, in the
hope she'd invite him in! And as she'd stood there, with
only a brief nightshirt to conceal her nakedness, her
hair tumbling untidily around her slim shoulders, he'd
had to restrain himself from gently leading her back into
the room and locking the door behind them! If he *had*
done such an outrageous thing, he knew very well the
reception he'd have got! This was not a run-of-the-mill
woman, and he had a sneaking suspicion that there was
a lot more to know about Ms Candida Greenway.

His eyes narrowed slightly. There was a certain aloofness about her which mystified him. Not frigidity—no. Never. Her distinctive artlessness merely disguised an obviously warm and sensuous nature—and he'd had plenty of practice at sizing up women. But he sensed an underlying emotional chasm between them which he found hard to explain. He wasn't used to being held at a distance. Women always fawned around him—some of which he liked, he admitted, but most of which went straight over his head. Since his disastrous marriage to Kelly, which had ended in divorce nine years earlier, women *per se* no longer interested him that much—other than as amusing playthings from time to time. He'd decided a long time ago that his fictional heroines would take the place of any real ones…not so expensive, not so demanding—and not so damned unpredictable! Still, he'd hang in with Candida for the time being—if nothing else, it would please Faith. But their association wouldn't last longer than *he* wanted it to.

'Where's Ella?' Candida asked, glancing at him over her shoulder as she went towards the window.

'In the kitchen, already snoozing after her supper,' Max said.

He'd put on a fresh cream open-neck shirt and dark trousers that made him look suave and casual at the same time, and had taken the trouble to brush his hair. Candida looked away, annoyed with herself. She didn't want to admit that she found him desirable. *Desire?* How could disdain turn into desire? She swallowed hard, realising that her brief, but highly coloured thoughts were being matched by the reddening of her cheeks.

It was magical looking over London, with all the

lights twinkling, and Candida gazed at the scene below. Max came over and stood close to her, and she automatically moved away. He stared down at her quizzically, aware of her reason for doing it, and for a few moments neither of them spoke.

Then, 'Shall we have a drink before we go down the road?' he murmured. 'Would you like a glass of wine—or a whisky?'

Candida smiled quickly. 'Oh—not whisky, thanks,' she said. 'But a small glass of white wine would be good. Thanks.'

He moved away and went over to the drinks cabinet, and presently they sat opposite each other at the window, Max idly swirling his whisky around in the glass so that the ice cubes clinked against the sides.

'I'm sure my sister will have told you something about me and my way of life,' he said, 'so I think it only fair that you tell me something about yours, don't you?'

'Faith never even mentioned you,' Candida said promptly. 'As a matter of fact, much of the time I was at Farmhouse Cottage it was only with the people doing the work… Faith visited from time to time, of course, but mostly she was away, staying somewhere with Emily. And I only ever saw Rick twice.' She smiled. 'We never got around to too much chatting—or gossiping, as I expect *you* would call it,' she added.

'Ah, yes, Emily,' he said, not responding to that last remark. 'She's "into everything" as they say, isn't she? Just as well to keep her out of the way of pots of paint and expensive curtain material.' He drank from his glass, and returned his gaze to the scene below. 'They're going to be fruit-picking at the weekend,' he said casually. 'So

I've been roped in to help. There are a large number of trees in that little orchard, aren't there? It'll take more than a few of us to gather it all in—even with Emmy's assistance.'

'Yes, I noticed it was all ripening wonderfully when I was there,' Candida replied.

'How about joining us and helping out?' he asked, without looking at her. 'Many hands make light work, don't they?'

Candida glanced at him quickly. Spending two weekends in a row with Max Seymour was not on her agenda! 'Oh—sorry—I'm already booked…girls' night out,' she lied. 'But, thanks anyway.' She sipped at her wine, looking away.

'Oh, don't thank me. It's just that I know Faith would love you to be there as well. I had visions of arriving at their place with you beside me as a nice surprise.'

Well, hard luck, Candida thought. He was obviously used to every other woman who happened to cross his path jumping at his every whim and suggestion. But she was not one of them! She couldn't help feeling like a fly trying to avoid a spider's web, and this time she was not going to get enmeshed.

Presently, they went downstairs in the lift, leaving the huge building behind, and began to stroll along the wide pavements. It was a blissfully warm night, and Candida felt upbeat for a second. This was an unexpected date, she reminded herself, so she might as well get the most out of it that she could!

'I hope you like French cuisine,' he said, holding her arm briefly as they paused to cross the road. 'This place we're going to—Edouard's—is almost too close to home, so I eat there regularly. I don't spend much time in my own kitchen, I'm afraid. I'm not one of these new men who cooks all the time.'

He looked down at her, and she glanced back quickly—she'd already sensed that he was no domestic animal!

'I love French food,' she said at once. 'In fact, living away from home has enlarged my perspective on many things. When I was growing up we ate very traditional dishes, and my father still does. When I tell him I've been to a Chinese or an Indian restaurant, he always asks me what's wrong with good old English roast beef or Welsh cawl.'

'I've never heard that word—' Max began, and Candida interrupted.

'Oh, it's a favourite dish with everyone. It's cooked on the top of the stove, like a stew.'

'D'you think I'd like it?' Max asked doubtfully.

Candida shrugged. 'Probably not—not if you like highly spiced, exotic foods. Which I think you do, by the sound of it.'

'Umm…"cawl"…' Max repeated slowly. 'The word has something of a sinister—ring about it. What's in it?'

Candida smiled to herself. This wasn't just idle chatter, she thought. He hadn't come across the word before, and he wanted to explore its meaning.

'It's made with Welsh lamb,' she explained, 'and leeks, and carrots and potatoes, and lots and lots of parsley. And salt and pepper. Oh…it's gorgeous!' she added. 'My father makes wonderful cawl. It's always what we have for dinner when I go home.'

He smiled at her enthusiasm. 'I must try it one day,'

he said. 'Perhaps you'll make me some, and I'll give you my verdict?'

Just then they came to the restaurant. Opening the door, Max went in before Candida down a narrow, rather uninspiring passageway. Even before they got to the dining room the audible chatter of relaxed voices could be heard—and the delicious smell wafting around the place made Candida hope that the service was prompt! Because by now her hunger had intensified to an almost unbearable pitch! As they went inside she saw that it was full of people sitting at small tables, all being served busily—and noisily—by white-aproned waiters who darted around with trays held high—the popping of wine corks adding to the undeniably continental flavour.

As soon as they were spotted, a middle-aged Frenchman—who Candida learned was the owner/manager—bustled forward to greet them.

'Ah…Monsieur Seymour…'

'Hi, Edouard,' Max said easily. 'Can you accommodate us tonight?'

The manager looked around him. 'Your usual table is occupied, but come—zees one will be just right for you and—your lady.' He looked at Candida as only a Frenchman could, and then back at Max, who grinned at him. The two men exchanged meaningful glances.

'I knew I could rely on you, Edouard,' he said. 'We've had a…longish journey, and are in need of a little relaxation.'

Edouard bowed briefly. 'Of course.' He pulled out a chair for Candida, who sat down and looked around her.

So this was where Max Seymour usually had his evening meal, she thought. It was a boisterous, good-natured place, with small candles glowing on every table, and in spite of all her misgivings she knew that she was going to be able to go with the flow, and sit the rest of the day out quite happily.

'I can recommend the fish—the sea bass in particular is always very good—but don't ask for chips. Chips is a dirty word in a French restaurant, I believe. They don't even offer French fries here—but sautéed potatoes are always available.'

'Oh, thank you so much for stopping me from making a *faux pas*,' Candida said sarcastically. 'I would hate Edouard to think that you were entertaining your country cousin this evening!' Didn't *everyone* know that chips were not part of French cuisine? she thought testily. Max's world and hers were miles apart, that was obvious, but he needn't be so patronising about it!

'Oh, Edouard wouldn't think that,' he said amiably, looking across at her, his expression holding her captive for a second. 'But he will be very curious as to who I've brought with me tonight. I almost always eat alone…and seldom with a lovely woman.' He smiled a slow, devastating smile. 'The French admire the female sex,' he said, 'and they're the first to recognise a desirable woman.' He paused. 'Edouard will already be envisaging the remainder of our evening together. The French are a race which do not have silly hang-ups about the most natural and exquisite act known to humankind.'

Candida stared at him blankly. 'Well, thanks for pointing out the small cultural differences between our races which you think I should know,' she said tartly. 'But Edouard shouldn't waste his imagination on me—better to stick to his cuisine,' she added, glancing back down at the menu. 'I'm not totally unaware of how the French tick, and I've been to France many times,' she went on airily—omitting to mention that her visits had been school exchange affairs, and that the only Frenchmen she'd ever actually been introduced to had been young brothers and friends of the host family! 'I'll have the sea bass—on your advice,' she said firmly, almost adding, And it'd better be good! 'With a salad, please.'

She put the menu down and sat back, looking across at him. If he thought that their evening was going to follow the manager's assumption, he was going to be unlucky. After Max had driven her home, the end of this 'business' date was going to be a very firm goodnight! she thought emphatically.

'Good choice,' Max said. 'I'll have the same.'

He beckoned to the waiter, adding a bottle of white wine to their order. The latter arrived almost immediately, and Candida watched as the waiter filled their glasses to the brim.

Max picked his up to drink, and waited for Candida to do the same. 'Cheers,' he said. 'And thanks for agreeing to help me choose stuff for the apartment. Also for coming with me this afternoon.' He paused. 'I naturally spend a great deal of time alone when I'm writing—that's unavoidable, and very necessary. But it's the car that bugs me. I just hate driving alone I don't have any problem with trains and planes,' he added. 'Just car journeys.' He frowned slightly. 'I can't explain it,' he added, before Candida could say anything. 'Probably some small incident hidden away in my childhood memory box has the answer.' He shrugged. 'Anyway—today has been good, so…thanks.'

After a few minutes, a small basket of freshly baked bread arrived, and Candida couldn't resist taking some, and spreading it liberally with butter.

'Oh, this is *so* good,' she said appreciatively as she munched.

'Everything is made on the premises,' Max said. 'So I'm sure you can appreciate why I don't bother doing anything for myself.'

Candida nodded, but thought, It's all very well for *you*! Who else could possibly afford to eat out at a place like this every night of the week? And the answer was—people like him…wealthy, fun and fancy-free, with no obvious commitments.

Presently, the rest of their meal arrived, and Max had been right. The fish was superb, and the fragrant lemon dressing on the salad so mouthwatering that Candida found it difficult not to take some more bread and mop it around her plate so as not to waste a scrap! But she didn't want Max to think of her as a peasant, with earthy table manners!

Presently, Max said, 'D'you eat pudding?' Without waiting for an answer, he went on, 'I'm going to insist that we both have Crêpes Suzette—and don't argue, because I know them to be absolutely delicious. I seldom indulge in sweet things myself,' he added, 'so please don't decline, or you'll be denying me a treat. I won't have any if you don't.'

What could she say? 'Oh…well, I think I'll have Crêpes Suzette, please,' she said, as if it had been her decision in the first place, and he smiled.

'Good! I'm glad we're in total agreement!'

It was getting late as they drank the last of their

coffee, and soon they left the restaurant, collected his car, and began the long journey back to Candida's flat. Candida was aware that Max seemed to be driving much more slowly than he had before…as if he didn't want to bring the evening to an end.

Echoing her thoughts, he said suddenly, without looking at her, 'I haven't enjoyed a working day as much as this one for a very long time. Tomorrow is going to seem very dull by comparison.'

Feeling warm and relaxed—and well-fed!—Candida said, 'It's been a somewhat eventful day for me, too—and that supper was fantastic. So, thanks again.' She sighed 'I don't think I'll be treated quite so generously again in a hurry…I'm usually offered a cup of tea!'

Eventually they turned into Candida's street, and on her instruction Max pulled up opposite number seven.

'I'm always relieved to see my poor old car in its parking space when I come home,' she said. 'Though I suppose no one would want it!' She bent forward to retrieve her belongings from the floor of the car, and Max switched off the engine.

'Now—don't ask me in for a nightcap, will you, Candida?' he teased. 'Because I'm certain it's already past your bedtime.'

She smiled across at him briefly, thinking that she'd be very reluctant to invite him in to her place, whatever the time was, because the comparison with his would be odious. She turned away to look up at the first floor, and suddenly a surprised gasp escaped her lips. Her hand went to her mouth. Max looked at her questioningly.

'What is it?' he asked, following her gaze.

'It's just…there's a light on in the flat. And *I* didn't

leave it on, that's for sure! Look—you can just see it through from the back.' She frowned. 'I think it's the strip light under one of the kitchen units.'

Max could see that she was concerned. 'Well, let's go and take a look, shall we?' he said easily.

Candida anxiously drew in her breath. 'I don't like the look of this,' she said. 'We've had intruders in the street recently, and we've been warned about locking everything up securely when we're away, or out at night. So I've been extra-vigilant…' She was clearly agitated, and Max touched her hand briefly.

'Come on,' he said firmly. 'There's only one way to find out if anyone's up there—and don't look so worried. There are two of us, remember?'

'Yes, but what if he has a knife—or a gun?' Candida said, her imagination already running riot.

'Hey, hang on a minute,' Max said. 'If there *is* someone there, it's more likely to be a teenage tearaway trying his luck.' He paused. 'I'll go in first, you stay behind…we'll take whoever it is by surprise.'

They let themselves into the building quietly, then crept up the stairs to Candida's entrance on the first floor. She was about to say something, but Max put his finger to his lips, taking the key from her and opening the door gently. They went noiselessly into the flat, and saw that Candida had been right—there was a light on in the kitchen…but the room was empty. They looked at each other without speaking, then Max opened each of the doors, one by one, while Candida kept very close behind him, aware that her heart was pumping with tension. Finally, he turned to look down at her.

'There's no one here at all, Candida,' he said, in a way

which immediately made her feel small and ridiculous. 'I'm afraid you must have left that light on yourself.' He paused. 'Go and have a good look around, and satisfy yourself that nobody has been here, and that nothing's been touched.'

As she scrutinised every corner of the flat, Candida began to feel very foolish. Max was right. She *must* have left that light on in the kitchen—though she was always so careful not to waste electricity, or waste anything. She'd been taught that from a very early age. She shrugged, and glanced up at him apologetically.

'Well, I'm sorry to have dragged you up here under false pretences,' she said at last. 'I'm not usually careless about leaving lights on.' She hesitated. 'The police have kept warning us lately that there's been some breaking and entering, and it can fuel the imagination, I'm afraid.'

Now, with every light on in the flat, her modest abode was laid bare before Max's perceptive gaze, and Candida felt herself cringing inwardly. There could be no comparison between her place and his, she thought. Then she was cross with herself. This was her home and, although no mansion, it was comfortable and cosy—and a darned sight tidier than *his*, she thought. So he could think what he liked.

Whatever his private thoughts were, Max said easily, 'You have a very nice place here, Candida—perfect for you. And in a good location.'

Well, I'm glad you approve, Candida thought, admitting reluctantly that his words sounded genuine enough.

Just then his mobile rang, and Max raised his eyes in surprise. It was late—getting on for midnight. 'I've a feeling I know who this is,' he said casually, as he answered it, then, 'Anthea! Hi! To what do I owe the pleasure? Long time, no see.' He grinned as he listened. 'Umm—I'm afraid I'm unavailable tonight, darling' he went on, turning away slightly from Candida as he spoke.

Feeling awkward, Candida drifted away into the kitchen, from where she could still easily hear what Max was saying. His words, and the mellow tone he was using, suggested that he and Anthea were very well acquainted!

'I promise we'll get together soon,' Max continued, his voice sultry and soothing. 'But at the moment I'm rather preoccupied—as you know.' There was a long pause as he continued listening. 'Did I say that? Oh— well, sorry! But, yes, I promise…I really will ring. Goodnight, Anthea… Yes—yes, of course… Love you, too… Goodnight. Sleep well.'

Snapping the phone shut, he joined Candida in the kitchen. 'Sorry about that,' he said. 'I do get these nuisance calls from time to time. Though not always this late.'

Candida looked up at him quickly. That had not seemed like a nuisance call to her. Anthea was obviously very well known to him, and the way the conversation had run in-dicated that she enjoyed rather more than a platonic friend-ship with Max Seymour! But the way he'd spoken of the woman was belittling, inconsequential. He had clearly been fobbing her off—perhaps because the lateness of the hour suggested that Anthea was the worse for drink! But still, his attitude had been derisive. He must have dozens of women fawning around him like that, Candida thought. And he obviously loved every minute of it.

Not knowing exactly what to do to bring the evening to an end, she said, 'Um…would you like a coffee—or a glass of wine?' Please say no, she thought.

He did, smiling down at her briefly. 'No, thanks, Candida. I feel I've absorbed enough of your time today already.' He turned to go, and Candida followed him to the top of the stairs. 'Don't bother to come down—I'll let myself out,' he said. 'You'll ring me in due course about the stuff for the flat?'

'Yes, I'll ring you,' she said quickly. At least he hadn't taken advantage of the situation and expected to stay the night, she thought—although his gaze *had* lingered on her big double bed just now!

He merely stood looking down at her, as if he was reading her mind, with a dark, enigmatic smile on his lips, then, 'Well, goodnight Candida,' he said softly, and without another word he went down the stairs, closing the street door quietly behind him.

Candida waited there for a few moments, her fists pressed to her cheeks. The intimate conversation he'd had with the woman on his phone, the way he had spoken, was a painful reminder of Grant—of the way he'd so easily hijacked Candida's life, had made her feel special. If only there had been some way of knowing that she was just one of a crowd of other young, gullible women, all under his spell. She and the Antheas of this world must be mad! She'd been such a fool, she chided herself angrily. A susceptible, pathetic, up-from-the-valleys fool! Well, she'd learned her lesson the hard way. And she would never again find herself in that position—with *any* man!

CHAPTER FIVE

EARLY the following morning, Candida tried to stop herself from emerging into a state of wakefulness. With her eyes still refusing to open, she was desperately trying to hold onto her dream before it dissolved into oblivion. A dream which had filled her with warmth... and undeniably passionate thoughts...

She had been dreaming about Anthea and Max. Dreaming about their relationship... But those off-hand words of his had somehow changed from indifference to soft, intimate murmurings. In the dream, she'd seen Max quite clearly, but the woman's face had seemed indistinct. Max had been cradling her in his arms, looking down at her, kissing her parted lips, her neck, and his hands had moved gently over her body, caressing her. The woman had stirred restlessly beneath his touch, and their combined sighs of pleasure had been audible, mesmerising...

Candida's heart was beating rapidly now, thumping with the kind of urgency and intensity she always experienced when something frightened or disturbed her, and suddenly, with a gasp of self-awareness, she sat bolt upright, automatically drawing her duvet around her shoulders protectively.

It had not been Anthea beneath Max's determined, athletic body…it had been *her*—Candida! It was she who had responded to his masculinity, his desire to possess her, and in that dream she had participated fully! She swallowed, trying to regulate her breathing. What was *wrong* with her? Was she as feeble as that…to fall— even in slumber—for the obvious charismatic charms of yet another purposeful male? A male for whom one woman would never be enough, would never satisfy his lusts. And who had readily confessed to being selfish and self-obsessed. A man who enjoyed the company of women for the obvious reason and nothing else.

Fully awake now, Candida threw the bedclothes from her and went into the bathroom, switching on the shower. She would stand there for longer than usual and wash away her thoughts—wash away the dream that had unsettled her and left her wallowing in her emotions.

Meanwhile, back at his apartment, Max sat staring moodily at his computer. As he'd said to Candida last night, he couldn't remember enjoying a day as much as he had yesterday for a very long time. He had felt totally relaxed, contented. Everything had slotted in perfectly with his wishes, and he accepted that Candida—this woman his sister had introduced him to—was solely the cause. He admitted that he just liked being with her…and that thought bothered him.

He'd passed that stage—a long time ago—of fancying any female enough to really want to get to know her. It always ended in tears—theirs, not his, he reassured himself. But he knew that it had always been his fault. The thrill of the chase was the best, the only part that intrigued him. After that it was the wearisome business of compromise, understanding, tolerance, and, yes…boredom! He'd become like the *Marie Celeste*, he thought, floating about aimlessly on emotional seas with no one on board, all other voyagers having been tossed over the side with untimely haste when things threatened to get out of his control.

But now the intensely niggling thought that wouldn't go away was that Candida was sticking to her story of not being interested in *him*! Not in that way. As if she had no special feelings for him at all! He'd never before met a woman who hadn't come on to him at the first snap of his fingers!

Glancing up suddenly at his bookshelves, one of his mother's titles caught his eye, and his expression darkened.

Well, Mother dear, he thought, I wonder what *you'd* make of your illustrious son's present state of mind But he knew the answer to that. 'If you want success, cut out everything unnecessary from your life!' That had always been her directive, uttered many times. Thinking of his parents—his tall, majestic and influential mother, his kind and submissive father—seemed to add to Max's feelings of depression. He knew himself to be feeling lower, less certain of things, of himself, than he had for a long time. He gritted his teeth. Please, Faith, stop interfering in my life, he implored silently. I don't need it… I don't need *her*!

What he *did* need were favourable reviews when his book came out next month, he thought grimly. Plus some inspiration to get him to the end of the next one, whose deadline was looming! *That* should focus his mind!

* * *

Three weeks later, Candida found herself once more at the door of the mansion apartment. She'd made the arrangement with Max's secretary, having first established that he would be away. She didn't want to see him again for a while, hoping that time would dampen her feelings—because, however hard she tried, she just couldn't get the man out of her mind. Now, today, she was merely visiting to take measurements, and she certainly didn't need him there for *that*. Perhaps she could delay it another couple of weeks before bringing him samples and swatches to choose from.

Janet, the middle-aged secretary, opened the door, and with a friendly smile she beckoned Candida inside cheerfully. 'Actually,' the woman said, 'I'm just off home—I only work mornings…' She lowered her voice, even though no one else was there. 'And, frankly, that's long enough at the moment! When there's a book coming out, Mr Seymour is best avoided!'

'Oh, well, thanks for waiting to let me in,' Candida said. 'I'll be quick—this won't take long.'

She worked her way around the rooms in question, deftly taking all the measurements and carefully noting the details down on her large notepad. Suddenly the entrance door was thrust open, and Max strode in, slamming it behind him. Candida nearly dropped everything she was holding in surprise.

'Oh, hello… I thought you were going to be away…' she faltered, staring up at him from her kneeling position on the floor.

'I was. I've come back,' he said, rather curtly. He turned to Janet, who was hovering in the doorway. 'You go on home, Janet—thanks for today.' He threw his bulging leather briefcase down on the sofa and went across to the drinks cabinet.

Janet departed promptly, while Candida concentrated—or tried to concentrate—on what she was doing, even though her hands were suddenly trembling. She had not seen Max dressed as he was today—in a dark formal suit, immaculate shirt and tie—and his hair, which seemed to have been trimmed recently, gleamed darkly in the early-afternoon sunlight. He looked the successful businessman that he was, and the effect was dynamic and alluring. Candida bent her head even closer to her pad, not wanting to look at him.

'Would you like a drink?' he asked. '*I'm* in need of a stiff whisky, even though I haven't eaten yet today.'

'Then why don't you?' Candida said, still not looking up.

'Why don't I what?'

'Have something to sustain you first,' she said patiently. 'I should have thought that was sensible,' she added.

He didn't reply for a moment, and she looked up quickly, to find him gazing down at her—which made her colour up. Why did she bother to give him any advice about how he looked after himself? she thought, embarrassment suddenly invading her senses. Today was totally different from that other occasion, when everything had been so laid-back and informal. She might as well wipe the memory of it from her mind *now*! And get back to business! Because it was clear that the mood which Janet had mentioned hadn't gone anywhere! Candida could almost feel his dark, brooding temperament over the considerable distance that separated them in this vast room

To her enormous surprise, he slid the glass door of the cabinet shut, and came over to stand beside her.

'Perhaps you're right,' he said. 'Though it's not quite the time for Edouard's, is it?'

Candida stiffened. Was he thinking about the time they'd sat there together? Or was he just imagining his regular corner table, where he ate alone? she wondered.

Taking a deep breath, she said lightly, 'Why don't you have an egg or some cheese here at home, for once.' She nearly added, Like most normal people do. But she stopped herself just in time, because something told her that the familiarity they'd enjoyed before wasn't going to be repeated. She'd better mind what she said, if this job was going to come to anything. He could cancel it—and her—any time he liked. She knew that only too well—and contracts were a bit thin on the ground at the moment, she admitted ruefully.

She got up then, so that they were standing close together, and moved to edge past him. But he put out his hand, touching her arm briefly for a second.

'Would you do it?' he said.

She frowned. 'Do what?'

'An egg or some cheese. Like you said. I'm too knackered to start manufacturing anything edible for myself—in fact, knowing my abilities, it wouldn't come into the edible category at all.' He paused. 'Have you heard of *anybody* who couldn't even boil an egg properly?' he said seriously.

Candida smiled, in spite of all her quaky misgivings about being here alone with him again. 'I shouldn't worry about that,' she said. 'As a matter of fact, it's well known to be one of the hardest things to do—to get the yolk soft and the white firm. It often turns out the other way around.'

'Oh, I *am* glad to hear that.' He paused. 'Two eggs twice, please,' he added.

'*Twice?*' Candida echoed. 'That'll be *four* eggs— too much all at once, for anyone.'

'Exactly. One helping each—one for you, and one for me.'

Candida looked at him blankly. He was at it again, she thought, arranging her next move to suit himself!

'Can't you *eat* alone, either?' she asked, in a way that was meant to remind him of his admission that he didn't like driving alone. He smiled at her, obviously taking the point.

'Oh, I'm not so hung up about that,' he said slowly. 'But I bet *you* haven't had lunch yet, either, have you?'

'No—o—' Candida said reluctantly. 'But I can wait.'

'If you eat with me, you won't have to,' he said, and Candida sighed inwardly. Things were going from bad to worse where this man was concerned. Every move she tried to make to distance herself from him, he made two more to foil her plans. He wasn't supposed to *be* here today at all!

But she knew she'd agree. Max seemed to have had a permanent influence on her life from their first moment together to the present day. It had been an unbelievable coincidence that had brought them together, face to face at last. How could she possibly have known that he would turn out to be the brother of Faith Dawson—or that she would be invited to a party and actually meet him, do work for him, spend time with him?

Together, they went into the beautiful kitchen, where

all the elaborate fitments gleamed with cleanliness—proving that very little cooking had ever gone on. But Candida had been preparing meals for herself and for her father for most of her life, and she soon found her way around the place, producing a light, nourishing lunch for them in next to no time. As she piled fluffy eggs onto toast, she wondered what her father—Freddy—would say if he could see her now. Even *being* in a place as amazing as this was something she'd never expected to do, but to be this close to someone famous, and preparing and eating lunch with him, would have impressed her unworldly father beyond words.

They ate with trays on their laps, sitting on the sofa in the window, and presently he said, 'Can I have my whisky now?'

'After coffee,' Candida said promptly, getting up and going back into the kitchen to make it.

They lounged in what could only be described as companionable silence, Max with his whisky in his hand, when, staring into the glass, he said suddenly, 'Well, those were the most damn-awful days I've had in a long time. I'm just thankful they're behind me—for now.'

Candida glanced at him, but decided not to ask him to explain. She sensed from the way he spoke that all he wanted was for someone to listen…not to interrupt and add any remark, but just to listen to what he wanted to say.

'It's all business, you know,' he said sullenly. 'The unutterably boring side of any commodity…*selling*.' He swigged from his glass. 'But that's not *my* problem! Why can't they just let me get on with what I'm good at? Writing the blasted stuff!'

Although Candida wasn't too sure what he was going

on about, she thought it probably had something to do with discussions with his publishers about future book signings—which she knew all famous authors did. She could just imagine how Max Seymour would hate that—having to smile at everyone, being asked to add dozens, possibly hundreds of personal messages inside the covers of his novels.

'I hate publicity and everything to do with it,' he went on vehemently. 'Plans are already in place for the next round of interminable journeys…for people to suck up to me and for me to suck up to them in the hope they'll keep buying my stuff.'

'Well, isn't that a small thing to do for success?' Candida asked coolly, thinking that *she* wouldn't object to having to do it! She'd jump at the chance!

'Oh, the first few times are OK,' he said morosely. 'But trailing around the country, visiting one shop after another, saying the same things…the novelty wears off in no time.'

There was silence for a moment as his words sank in, and Candida suddenly felt thoroughly antagonised. She stared across at him coldly.

'That's pathetic,' she said. 'No—I'll rephrase that. *You're* pathetic!'

He returned her look. 'What d'you mean—I'm pathetic?' He sat forward, obviously stung by her comment.

'I mean that spending a comparatively short time in your oh, so important life being gracious for a few hours, showing your appreciation to your buying public, should be the very *least* you can do! Your books aren't cheap—even the paperbacks cost enough! And to have one with the author's signature and a short message makes them a bit special.' She paused, swallowing. 'It makes the buyer think that you actually *value* their loyalty!'

His arrogant outlook on the matter had really got to Candida now. 'But don't worry,' she added hotly. 'You're never likely to see *me* in a queue waiting to receive your condescending scribble!'

Max's expression had darkened at her outburst, and for a moment it looked as if he didn't know what to say.

'There are *bound* to be down sides in every occupation,' Candida said, speaking more quietly. 'My own clients are usually very reasonable people, but occasionally I get those who keep changing their minds, or disagree with all my suggestions, and some never give any hint of appreciation of all the efforts I've made on their behalf, even though I've bent over backwards to obtain exactly what they wanted.' She turned to look at him, her eyes glistening with intensity. 'Do you know, I occasionally have to increase my overdraft to pay my bills, until these often very wealthy clients decide to settle their accounts?' There, she thought. That was something she never discussed with anyone. But she wanted this egotistical man to realise that he wasn't the only one with problems!

There was silence for a few moments, and then he sighed, a long drawn-out sigh, staring stonily ahead of him. Candida, calming down somewhat, began to feel slightly uneasy. This was a very different Maximus Seymour from the one she thought she knew. In a minute, she thought, he was going to tell her to get out and never darken his doorstep again!

She got up decisively and glanced down at him.

There was something about his appearance that made him suddenly look like a lost little boy—although a very overgrown one! His hair was tousled from having run his hands through it several times, and he was tired and dispirited—that was plain enough. But there was something else…a deeper melancholy which hadn't been apparent before.

After a moment, she said, 'I must be going…I've taken all the measurements I need, and—'

Just then the doorbell rang, and without even bothering to get up, Max raised one dark eyebrow.

'Get that before you go… See who it is, Candida,' he said casually, and she stared at him. Who did this man think he was?

'No,' she said flatly. 'I think *you* should see who it is. I've got to collect my things together.' And with that she walked into the kitchen, where she'd left her belongings, while Max got up to answer the door.

It was a woman, and the shrill, imperious voice resounded through the high-ceilinged apartment.

'Max! Darling! You don't mind me dropping by, do you? I'm absolutely *shattered*…shopping since dawn! I knew you'd be home this afternoon, and I hope you haven't drunk all your whisky because I'm in desperate, *desperate* need…'

Candida wondered if there was a back way out of this place, or a fire escape she could run down. Because for some reason she had no wish to meet the owner of those high-pitched tones! But she knew she was trapped, and Max's voice—not as enthusiastic-sounding as his caller's—interrupted.

'*Hello*, Fiona! Of course—do come in.' And with

barely a pause he added, 'You're not my first visitor today…you must meet my newest find. A young lady of outstanding abilities.' He called out to Candida. 'Candida—do come and meet Fiona…' As Candida reluctantly emerged from the kitchen, he said to the woman, 'Candida is an interior designer who's going to smarten things up a bit for me here.'

Fiona was tall, raven-haired and glamorous, of about Max's age, Candida thought as they were introduced.

Max smiled down at her briefly. 'Fiona works for my agent,' he explained. 'As we all must do,' he added somewhat ruefully.

The woman stared down at Candida, making no effort to disguise the fact that she was assessing Max Seymour's 'newest find'—a description which Candida had heard only too clearly, and which had made her feel like some sort of throwaway commodity. *He* hadn't found her, in any case, she thought, it was his sister's doing that had brought them all together.

'Well, well—good to meet you,' the older woman drawled, putting down the numerous bulging glossy carrier bags she'd been holding, while still examining every aspect of Candida's appearance. And Candida cringed. She always wore jeans, and a white top of some sort when she was working, with her hair tied back in a ponytail, out of harm's way. But Fiona was immaculate, in a sharp black suit and an expensive, broad-striped satin shirt, her long legs encased in sheer dark stockings. And she was wearing pointed-toed shoes with the highest heels Candida had ever seen. Her hair, swept back off her forehead and coiled into an extravagant bun, exposed strong features, which Candida felt instinctively would reflect every passing mood—especially discontented, irritable ones. But now the bright red fulsome lips were set in a half-smile—which didn't exactly convince Candida that *her* presence was appreciated!

Max broke the brief silence. 'You've had an expensive morning,' he observed dryly, glancing down at Fiona's shopping.

'Oh—you know me, darling. Only too well!' the woman replied, going over and resting her head briefly against his shoulder. Then she looked across at Candida. 'I do hope I'm not holding up the good work here…'

'No, not at all,' Candida said hastily, suddenly desperate to get away. 'I've finished for now.' Then, turning to Max, she said, 'As soon as I've got the samples to hand, I'll ring your secretary to make another appointment.'

She went towards the door, but Max barred her way. 'Would you like to stay for a cup of tea?'

'Oh, don't delay the poor working girl!' Fiona exclaimed. 'I'm perfectly capable of making us some tea—I know my way around your kitchen better than anyone…I've had plenty of practice, goodness knows!' she added, shooting a smug little smile in Candida's direction before going over to the window, kicking off her shoes as she went.

Candida glanced at Max—who seemed to have cheered up considerably, she noticed. But why not? His life must be overrun by women like this one…with his wealth and good-looks he must attract them like flies. And like all men—well, like the only man *she'd* ever had any real experience with—he'd lap it up, make the most of every opportunity. Her eye caught Fiona's discarded shoes for a second. No doubt Max would move into foot treatment mode as soon as the two of them were left together, she thought, remembering only too well the feel of his hands manipulating her toes at Faith's party, remembering how his palms had encased each of her feet in turn, massaging them with a strength and firmness that even now made her tingle…

She turned determinedly to leave. There was no place for her here!

'Well—goodbye…' she said, rather awkwardly. 'Good to have met you, Fiona…'

Max stopped her for a second. 'Just wait a minute while I get those details we were discussing,' he said, and Candida watched him disappear into his study, not knowing what on earth he was talking about.

In a moment or two he came back and thrust a small envelope into her hand, and then at last, thankfully, Candida was allowed to make her departure.

With her cheeks flaming at her own sense of irrelevance—thanks to the overpoweringly sophisticated and rather supercilious Fiona—Candida made her way along the street. Well, the woman's whole persona and attitude was no surprise, was it? she asked herself. Just the sort of creature she'd have imagined Max enjoying spending time with—and not only in business, either. As had been made abundantly clear! Candida wondered how they'd be spending the rest of the day, alone there in his apartment… Then she tried to shut out her thoughts. She didn't want to imagine them! She wanted to forget them!

Later, as the tube rocked and lurched its way beneath town, Candida felt in her pocket for Max's 'details', curious as to what he'd meant. Opening the slip of paper, she read, 'I'll ring you first thing in the morning. Keep the day free.'

And that was it. Candida turned the paper over to see if there was something on the other side, but there wasn't. She had to be satisfied with one short statement, and the command which followed it.

Replacing it in her pocket, Candida let her thoughts return to Fiona. How many of those women *were* there? she asked herself. So far, she was aware of only two, but clearly Max enjoyed playing the field, putting himself about—and there would be no shortage of supply.

Staring blankly at the notices and advertisements above her, Candida set her lips in a straight, determined line. The note left her in no doubt that she was being required to fall in with more of Max Seymour's plans tomorrow—but she was *definitely* not going to be coerced. Let him amuse himself with those other females. Their world and hers bore no comparison, she thought. She was not in their bracket and would never be. Nor would she want to be.

She sighed, suddenly feeling lost and a bit homesick. Tonight she'd ring her father and have a good, long chat. That should put everything neatly back into perspective.

CHAPTER SIX

THE next day—Saturday—Candida, still in her dressing gown, stood in the kitchen making her breakfast toast and coffee. Last night, she'd been on the phone to her father for a whole hour, and his cheerful no-nonsense opinions on the hundred and one topics they'd chatted about had filled Candida with a wonderful sense of normality. That was the kind of life she was used to—with people like him. People she understood and loved, she thought. She wished her father would make the journey to London more often, but she knew that, apart from being in the company of his adored daughter, the place held little attraction for him. During their long chat last night she'd almost managed to forget Max Seymour and his illustrious women friends. Well—almost! There *was* just the small matter of the note he'd given her yesterday. He said he'd ring, and she knew that he would. And the bit about keeping the day free was unequivocal, too. Well, we'll see about that, she thought.

Swallowing the last of her orange juice, Candida went into the bathroom. Saturdays were always reserved for a long, lazy soak, part of a rather simple routine which she didn't like interrupted.

She hadn't even got as far as turning on the taps when the phone rang, and the colour automatically rushed to her cheeks. She waited a second before picking up the receiver.

'Good morning to you, Candida.' The familiar throaty voice met her ears, but before she could say anything, he went on, 'I've thought of a rather good idea for today. I hope you'll think so.'

'Oh—hi,' Candida said airily. 'And what idea is that?'

'Well, it's for Ella, really,' he went on. 'When I collected her from the Jarretts later on yesterday, she seemed a bit withdrawn—kind of sorry for herself. And, as I'd been away for nearly a week this time, I thought I owed her a treat to make up for it.'

Well, go and give her a treat, then, Candida thought. Why should it concern *her*?

'It's a gorgeous morning, and a wonderful day for a picnic,' he said coolly. 'I thought we could drive out to the country somewhere, take our lunch, and have a good long walk. It'd do us all good. This weather can't hold for ever—we should make the most of it.'

Candida found it hard to get her thoughts in order. Hearing his voice again, and being asked to spend yet more time with him, was threatening to undo all the good that talking to her father had achieved. Last night she'd started to feel less tense, to feel that there was life outside the clutches of Max Seymour, but now…

'Oh, sorry…I don't think I can come. I'm just about to have a bath—' she began.

'No problem,' he interrupted. 'Just say when you'll be ready, and we'll come and fetch you. Whatever time you like.'

Candida felt an irritated helplessness sweep over her. It just did not occur to him that she might not *want* to go with him—anywhere! Let him ask one of his other women, she thought. 'Can't Fiona go with you? Can't she do the honours?' she asked, trying not to sound sarcastic. She didn't imagine that picnicking and rambling would be quite to the woman's taste. Especially with *her* feet—which Candida had immediately noticed were starting to show the first signs of bunions. There was nothing sexy about bunions!

'Why should I ask her?' Max said.

'Well, I'm sure she'd be a far more…satisfying… companion than me. You've…you've so much in common, after all.'

'You think so?' He paused. 'Fiona doesn't like dogs, so that's no good. Besides, she's abroad until Monday,' he went on, unperturbed. 'I was thinking of you, not her. I thought that what I had in mind would be right up your street.'

So it was *her* that he was thinking about…not himself! That was a first!

She dug in her heels. 'No—I haven't had any time to do food shopping this week yet. There's nothing exciting in the fridge, and—'

'Oh, don't worry about that,' he said quickly. 'I've already been over to the deli and ordered our picnic— which they're preparing as we speak.' He waited before going on. 'They do the most wonderful hampers,' he added.

Candida shook her head in disbelief. He'd been so sure of himself—so sure she'd agree to fall in with his wishes that he'd already sorted out the picnic! Well, tell him to get lost then, she told herself savagely. She had begun the day so determined not to spend any more time than was absolutely necessary with the man, yet here she was, already having difficulty not buckling beneath his lordly plans! Biting her lip, she sent a panicky message to her guardian angel. But…but it *was* a beautiful day, and the thought of a few hours in the countryside, especially with the dog, suddenly became overwhelming.

Why not take advantage of this opportunity? she asked herself. Only a fool would turn down the chance of being driven in that fabulous car—with a no-doubt gourmet meal thrown in for good measure. Surely she could do herself no harm in accompanying him today? she thought. There was nothing else on the immediate horizon, so she might as well grab this with both hands and stop agonising.

'Oh, all right, then,' she said casually. 'But I can't be ready before eleven.'

'That's fine by me, Candida,' he said evenly.

They rang off and, glancing at the clock, Candida saw that it was already nine-thirty. The usual long soak in the bath would have to be a more hurried affair, she thought. But the weather promised to be even warmer than it had been recently, so the choice of what to wear was not difficult. Her favourite narrow-leg cream trousers, teamed with an expensive tan and white striped sports shirt seemed right—she always felt good in the casual, up-to-the-minute outfit—and her trusty loafers would stand her in good stead for the proposed walk.

Quickly, she blow-dried her hair, which she decided to leave loose, then moisturised her face, before adding a light touch of foundation and blusher. Right, she thought, her chauffeur could arrive any time he liked!

A short, distinctive blast on the car horn made Candida smile briefly as she glanced out of the window. Eleven on the dot.

Picking up her pretty summer holdall, she ran lightly down the stairs, feeling quite pleased, now, to be going somewhere a bit special on a Saturday. Max had got out of the car, and came around to her side to open the door for her. He looked at her appreciatively, pausing for a second.

'You look…wonderful,' he said. He gazed down at her in a way which made her stomach turn somersaults, and she smiled up at him briefly, trying not to let his words mean anything more than the predictable comment he, or any man, might make to a woman. But the way Max had uttered them was different, she thought instinctively. And he was not the sort to say *anything* he didn't mean! And, to make things worse, he looked more stunningly handsome than ever today, dressed in casual white trousers and a navy polo shirt. He handed her into the car, then got in beside her, and they set off, with Ella lying contentedly on her rug on the back seat, her tail wagging gently.

'Hello, Ella!' Candida turned around and leaned over to smooth the dog's head. The animal slowly got up in response.

'Sit, Ella!' Max's stern command had the desired effect, and Ella immediately flopped back down, still keeping her large brown eyes fixed on Candida.

'Very impressive,' Candida said, shooting a glance at Max. 'Obviously one word from you and she does as she's told…'

Max grinned across at her, his blue-black eyes even deeper than the colour of his shirt. 'But naturally. All my women do exactly as I tell them,' he said, returning his attention to the road.

'Oh…really?' Candida said lightly. 'Yeah, right!'

'Well,' he drawled, and there was laughter in his voice, 'I get the occasional dissenter, of course. But they come around to my way of thinking in the end.'

Candida decided not to continue with this dialogue— he was deliberately being provocative, and she was not going to take the bait! Looking across at him quickly, she wondered whether he had forgotten about how she'd left him in no doubt as to what she thought of his arrogant attitude towards his devoted readers. But then the lovely Fiona would have smoothed over any minuscule dent which might have upset his masculine sense of superiority, she thought. How long had the woman stayed? Candida wondered. Had they gone to Edouard's for supper and, later on, shared Max's king-size bed?

Candida wanted to kick herself—who *cared*, whatever they did?

She made herself stop this flow of thoughts, and sat back to enjoy the ride.

Max obviously knew exactly where he was taking them, because they were soon clear of the motorway. Candida closed her eyes. She was determined to enjoy the day for what it was going to be: a simple picnic in the English countryside.

It was twelve-thirty before they reached their destination—a place clearly familiar to Max because, after driving up a steep hill and along a side road for a mile or two, he pulled onto a grassy lay-by surrounded by tall trees, which offered the most glorious view of rolling hills and the valley below them.

He stopped the car, and at the touch of a button the windows slid open and the scent of fading summer drifted in, making Candida's nostrils tingle with familiar nostalgia.

'Oh,' she murmured, 'this is…wonderful! What a fantastic spot!'

'I thought it might please you,' he said. 'But you must know similar places in your own neck of the woods—at home in Wales, I mean.'

'Oh, yes, of course,' Candida said at once. She hesitated. 'I do miss all that…you know, being able to go out of the house, down the path, across the road and over the stile…and to just ramble for miles over the fields.' She sighed. 'But you can't have everything, can you? I live a different life now.'

Max opened the door to let Ella out of the car, and the dog jumped down eagerly and began sniffing around the banks. Candida got out too, and reached into her bag for her sunglasses. Then she stood beside Max, and the two of them gazed at the scene rolling away from them.

'Well, maybe all that will be possible some time in the future,' he said easily. 'Perhaps you won't always have to live so near London.'

'Perhaps,' Candida agreed. 'But, as I've said, here is where big money is spent. I don't think I'd have as many clients at home who'd have the sort of resources to pay what I earn here.'

'Even if some of them do take their time in coughing up?' Max said, and Candida shot him a quick glance. He *had* remembered what they'd been talking about yesterday, she thought And there was certainly no way he'd have forgotten her uncomplimentary opinions!

He opened the boot of the car and took out a bottle of water and a metal drinking bowl, which he filled to the brim.

'Here, Ella,' he said, and the dog trotted over and began lapping thirstily.

Max glanced across at Candida. 'It is time for lunch, but…' He paused. 'D'you want to eat straight away? The day's our own.'

'I'd love a stroll first,' Candida replied.

'Fine. We'll work up an appetite,' he said at once. He picked up Ella's empty drinking bowl and replaced it in the car before locking up. 'This way,' he said, nodding in the direction they were to take, and together they set off, the dog bounding on a little way ahead.

'How old is Ella?' Candida asked.

'Nearly three,' Max replied. 'And I can't imagine life without her now.'

'Yes. Dogs do that to you, don't they?' Candida said. 'She's in wonderful condition—you must be giving her a very happy life.'

'Oh, I always value my belongings,' he said. 'And I wouldn't dream of neglecting any female—they're far too essential a component in the grand scheme of things.'

He looked down quizzically at her as they walked side by side, but she refused to return his gaze. He was clever with words, she thought—and why not? They were what earned him his fabulous lifestyle. She decided to change the subject—and maybe at last give herself the opportunity to mention the thing that was on her mind.

'When did you first know you wanted to write pro-fessionally, Max? To be an author?' she asked innocently.

'Oh—can't remember…it was too long ago,' he said abruptly, looking away. 'From the day I could actually form a sentence, I suppose. There were always pens and writing material available, naturally.'

Candida nodded. 'I suppose your mother's influence had a lot to do with it?' she suggested, and was surprised by his rather curt reply.

'Oh, you could say that,' he said brusquely. He paused for a second. 'Look—I reckon we can probably see fifty, sixty, seventy miles in every direction from here. Isn't that…doesn't that give you a feeling of…release? Of freedom from a world outside yourself and the pettiness of life?'

Candida glanced up at him. For a few seconds he was in a world of his own, she thought, noticing that fleeting 'lost' look about him that she'd observed before.

They continued walking for a couple of miles without saying much, the sun hot on their backs, and presently Candida paused for a second, pushing her sunglasses on to the top of her head and touching the bridge of her nose with a tissue.

'Wow,' she said, 'it really is a warm day.'

'We'll sit down for a bit,' he said, immediately going across to a raised grassy stump. 'This looks reasonably comfortable.' He eased himself into a sitting position, his long legs stretched in front of him, and held his hand out towards Candida. After a moment's hesitation she took it, and they sat there together, with Ella trying to nose her way between them.

Candida suddenly felt an undeniable surge of well-being sweep over her, and she turned to look at Max. 'This was a great idea of yours, Max,' she said. 'To come out for the day. It beats supermarket-shopping and cleaning the flat!'

He smiled, a long, lazy smile, his smouldering eyes seeming to burn their way right into her soul, and, however much she tried, Candida couldn't look away.

'I'm known for my great ideas,' he said casually.

There were several moments of complete silence as he stared at her. Then, 'And, by the way, I realise that sunglasses are useful things, but they obscure the eyes…and yours are too lovely to remain hidden.' He paused. 'Where did you get them from?'

Candida felt herself blushing at the compliment. Although her mother had been considered beautiful, she knew it was her father's dark eyes she'd inherited, fringed as they were by long, naturally curling lashes. But, pleasant though it was to have such a heart-throb member of the opposite sex say such things, Candida was not going to take his words too seriously. He always knew exactly what to say in any given situation, and it obviously amused him to flatter the woman he was with.

'I ordered these specially—on my birthday,' she said lightly, in answer to his question. 'And, talking of eyes—where did you get yours? Which of your parents do you resemble?'

'Never thought about it,' he said. He glanced at his watch. 'Come on, I'm beginning to get hungry.'

They resumed their walk, and presently got back to the car.

'How far did we go?' Candid asked.

'Oh, that was no more than a three-mile round trip,'

Max replied, leaning into the boot. He lifted out a picnic hamper and set it down on the grass next to a moss-covered stony boulder, where he promptly sat down, patting the place beside him.

'We seem to be destined to sit together at meal times, Candida,' he said, opening the hamper and taking out a bottle of red wine. 'I don't know whether all this will come up to Edouard's standard, or my sister's party, for that matter, but it will have to do.'

'Having to do' was a slight understatement, Candida thought, as the contents of the deli picnic were unwrapped, all the food having been surrounded by ice packs to keep it cool and fresh.

Candida set out delicately garnished finger rolls on a plate, adding miniature pork pies, pickled eggs and cherry tomatoes. Accompanied by a box of celery, cucumber and avocado salad, with a segmented bowl of different savoury dips, it was a gastronomic banquet fit for royalty.

'Where do we *start*?' Candida asked appreciatively. 'We'll never get through all this.'

'We start right now—and don't bank on there being much left. I'm starving,' he replied.

He poured wine into two glasses, and held one out to Candida. 'See how you like this,' he said. 'I always buy it for special occasions.'

Candida decided to ignore yet another of his smooth compliments, which were impressing her less every time he made one, but as soon as the velvety liquid touched her tongue she knew it to be of the highest quality. But *naturally*! she thought!

'Umm—nice,' was all she said.

Max drank freely from his glass, before putting food onto his plate, then leant back on one elbow as he chewed. The dog lay down a little way away, watching the proceedings, but not attempting to get up.

'Is Ella allowed something?' Candida asked, about to share her piece of pie.

'Certainly not,' was the prompt reply. 'She'll have her meal at suppertime, not before.'

Candida made an apologetic face. 'Oops—sorry I spoke,' she said lightly. 'I'm afraid our Toby eats rather more often than that.'

'And is Toby overweight?'

'Um…I suppose he is inclined to be fat,' Candida admitted.

'There you go, then,' was the laconic reply.

Presently, he said, 'You asked me about my writing…' He drank from his glass. 'Have you ever been interested yourself?' His lip curled. 'Most people are said to have a book inside them somewhere—d'you fall into that category?'

Candida could hardly believe her ears! This was surely the opportunity she'd never thought would come her way! The perfect moment to say—Yes, I *did* write a book once, Max, published by a small independent firm who could ill afford rotten notices, and you put your destructive heel right on it, and on *me*. And I haven't *dared* to go down that road again! Nor ever shall! Go on, go on…say it! *Tell* him, she said to herself fiercely. See what effect it has—if any!

Her heart was beating so rapidly now that she could barely swallow the small piece of roll she'd been eating, and he looked across at her, waiting for her to reply to his question. Perceptive as ever, he noticed her change of expression, and he frowned slightly.

'Is everything…OK, Candida?' he asked, and she smiled quickly, trying to cover her confusion.

Why spoil this perfect day? she asked herself. It was such a blissful occasion—how could she put a damper on it? Especially with Ella lying there looking at them both so adoringly. No…*one* day there would be just the right time—she was sure of it—but this was not it!

'Everything is…wonderful, thanks,' she replied lightly, surprised and a bit disappointed, at her own cowardice. 'I'm—really enjoying myself,' she said simply.

For a long, timeless moment, he looked at her, then slowly he put down his glass and plate and took hers from her. He leaned across, and Candida knew what he was about to do. Knew what was going to happen. And there wasn't anything she could do about it. There wasn't anything she *wanted* to do about it!

Gently, he pulled her towards him, looking deep into her eyes, searching her expression, and Candida was aware of a feeling of light-headedness, of floating, almost, as she gazed back at him. She was caught like an animal in the glare of a headlight, transfixed by the dark, passionate message from his mesmerising eyes….and then their lips met—not in a hungry, devouringly passionate way, but in a total embrace of two sensitive human beings melding together, wanting to become one in fleshly contact.

The feel of his mouth on hers immediately left Candida's senses swimming with desire, and, recognising this at once, Max responded to it with masterful and well-practised ease, his masculinity springing to life with an urgency that actually took him by surprise. He held her to him even more closely, the moistness of their parted lips meeting, fusing, enthralling them. Candida's long lashes fluttered gently on the soft curve of her cheek as she allowed herself to lapse into a temporarily drugged state of sexual longing, and Max's heart thudded vigorously in his chest, matching the rapid pulse of this woman whom he wanted to possess at this moment, more than anything he'd ever wanted in his whole life. Knowing instinctively that she was ready for him, ready for love, he gently slid his hand into the open neck of her shirt, the soft warmth of her perfect rounded breast beneath his palm filling him with anticipation…

Then, without warning, she pulled away, her eyes like those of a startled animal. 'No. *No*, Max,' she said quickly, and he saw that she was shaking. 'I'm sorry— but no,' she said, looking away from him.

Max cursed inwardly, but was not surprised. He'd known from the beginning that this woman was a one-off, and he knew he had a long way to go before she fell in with his plans! If he *ever* managed it!

Controlling himself with a supreme effort, he eased away from her and took up his wine glass. 'Told you this was good stuff,' he said, aiming at jocularity, even though jocularity wasn't the word he wanted to use at this moment!

For a few minutes they didn't say much as they resumed their meal, and then, to break the silence, Candida said unexpectedly, 'Do you know what I'd *really* like to do now?'

He looked at her quickly—hopefully—but didn't think for a second that her wishes matched his present erotic ones! 'Whatever the lady requires…' he murmured.

'It's *ages* since I went blackberrying,' she said. 'It's exactly the right time of year, and there are bound to be lots of them ripe with the summer we've had.'

Sighing, but smiling in spite of himself, Max got up. 'That's an easy wish to grant,' he said. 'If we go down to the railway line, there are hundreds of bushes there—if they haven't already been stripped. It won't take us long.'

He pulled her to her feet, and Candida had to fight the emotional surge that ran through her body yet again. This picnic hadn't been such a good idea after all, she thought. But she was glad—glad—that she'd rejected his advances just now. It had been a near thing, but she'd managed it…somehow. She had the painful legacy of two-timing Grant to thank for that! D for Desire, Danger, Disillusionment, she reminded herself.

Together, they cleared the remains of the picnic, re-placing everything in the boot of the car, and Candida reached into the passenger side to retrieve her holdall.

'I've always got some plastic bags handy,' she said, as she took them out. 'They'll do for putting the fruit in.' She looked up at him, suddenly feeling a bit awkward about their close encounter earlier. 'Do you mind very much…? I mean…do you like blackberrying?'

'Dunno. Never done it,' he said. He looked down at her, his dark eyes trying to analyse her thoughts, trying to understand this woman, this unusual woman. What *was* it with her? he asked himself, still trying to quench his frustration. Perhaps she didn't like his choice of after-shave! Then he shrugged inwardly. He'd find out—one way or another. 'But—there's a first time for everything,' he said, in answer to her question, 'and I'm not known for turning down any new and exciting opportunity!'

CHAPTER SEVEN

TOGETHER the three of them made their way towards the railway line, Ella running ahead. It was, in fact, much further away from their picnic spot than Max had indicated, with a couple of wide fields, small copses, and a brook with no more than a trickle of water in it to be negotiated. But at last they made it, and there were plenty of blackberry bushes in evidence.

Feeling hot, but exhilarated, Candida looked up at Max as they took stock of the situation. 'You were right, Max—someone's been here before us,' she said. 'But look at all those blackberries on the top stems—still plenty left for us if we can reach them.'

He grinned down at her, realising that he felt as energised as she looked—and also aware that their relationship seemed to have taken a more encouraging turn. It was true that she had resisted him earlier, but he had not been able to help himself—and he wasn't sorry that he'd done it. It had been a simple matter of the desire of a full-blooded male for a tantalizingly beautiful woman, and she'd demonstrated a sensual side to her nature that had excited and invigorated him in an unexpected way. It had been something of a delightful surprise! And one which gave him some grounds for thinking that their…. association…might develop into something more satisfying to him.

He glanced up at the top bushes. 'I think I can get most of those,' he said, shielding his eyes against the lowering autumn sun. 'Especially if we can find a longish stick to help grab them.' He peered around him, treading the grass underfoot, and as if fate had arranged it a conveniently sized branch with a bit of a gnarled hook at the end presented itself. 'Ah—this'll do,' he said, picking it up.

In the end there were still enough blackberries at the base of the bushes for Candida to nearly fill her plastic bag, while Max continued reaching up to pick the huge, luscious ones at the top, his powerful height barely needing the branch he'd found. He looked down at her as she crouched to pick the berries almost at ground level, and stopped what he was doing to stare at her for a second or two. Her hair floated luxuriously around her shoulders, reminding him of the advertisements he'd seen on TV for hair colourants. Except he knew instinctively that the rich darkness of Candida's was purely what nature had endowed her with.

She sensed him looking at her, and as their eyes met he was rewarded by a certain something in her expression that told him most of what he wanted to know. She was as attracted to him as he was to her, and for the moment that had to be enough. But the best was yet to come, he reassured himself—if he could overcome whatever it was that seemed in the way. His brows knitted fleetingly… Somehow he didn't feel that she was playing hard to get, or making herself deliberately elusive and distant from him—there was something much deeper than that. And that was what he had to discover!

She smiled up at him. 'How're you doing?' she asked. Then, 'I'm glad you're here, because the best fruit is always just out of reach—and that's what makes it all the more irresistible, isn't it?'

'Probably a good allegory for life in general, don't you think?' he asked, one eyebrow lifting quizzically.

Candida looked away quickly. 'Probably,' she agreed.

Getting up, she scrutinised her bag of blackberries. 'Well, I've done rather well—though mine will be much smaller specimens than yours, obviously.' She looked up at him again. 'I'm sure we don't need any more—you can stop now, Max.'

'Thanks very much,' he replied dryly.

'I'll be able to make several apple and blackberry tarts with what we've picked,' Candida said contentedly. 'A couple for you, a couple for me, and some for Dad. He loves home-made pies and things.'

'I can't ever remember having home-made apple and blackberry tart,' Max said, moving over to join her. 'My mother certainly never did any cooking, and anyway I seldom indulge in puddings—though Faith's always look wonderful when I eat there. I'm sure it's delicious.' He paused. 'Perhaps we'll have one together, after we've eaten that Welsh cawl stuff you told me about.'

Candida looked away for a minute, then suddenly espied a cluster of five huge berries, right inside the middle of the bush she'd just been picking from. 'Oh, look,' she said. 'I'll just get those, then we're done.'

Turning and bending forward, she extended her arm as far as she could, leaning in slightly to remove the berries from the stem, and then, without warning, she completely lost her balance and toppled over, falling headlong right into the centre—but still managing to hold on to her precious bag of fruit.

'Ow!' she yelled, as she felt the thorny stems scratch her spitefully. 'Ow, Ow, Ow!'

Immediately Max lunged towards her and grabbed her shoulders before she could fall any further, then pulled her back towards him. 'You see—you weren't satisfied,' he chided teasingly as he held her against him. 'That was the forbidden fruit that Eve knew all about in the Garden of Eden! You were not meant to have those, Candida!'

They were held together now in a tight embrace, and, looking down into her upturned face, his eyes were suddenly full of concern. 'Hey, Candida—you've really hurt yourself,' he said.

'Yes, and I didn't even manage to get the things I was reaching for either,' she said ruefully.

Putting down the bags of fruit, they examined the damage to Candida's skin. By now, thin streaks of blood began identifying the vicious scratches which were showing in several places on the back of her hands, wrists and lower arms. But, worse, an ugly red mark ran the length of one of her cheeks right down to her chin

She was stinging painfully from every wound—but feeling more ridiculous than sorry for herself. Why had she been so intent on getting those last few berries? she asked herself. She knew that she must be looking a terrible sight—bloody, grubby and dishevelled!

But Max, gazing down into her upturned face, didn't seem to see anything but her desirability, and, holding her to him again with his hands clasped at the base of her spine, he kissed the bruised cheek gently. Then, after a long moment, he took both her hands in his, touching his lips along the marks which were becoming angrier-looking with every second. 'Poor you,' he murmured. 'You didn't deserve that.' And, looking deep into her eyes, he claimed Candida's mouth in a lingering, longing kiss—not only in sympathy for the discomfort she was obviously feeling, but in a further display of his passionate need of her. Relaxing helplessly into him, Candida let him do it, let him empathise with her and console her…but most of all let him tune in to her own longing—the longing to be wanted, cherished, and, yes, *lusted* for! Feelings which she'd convinced herself she had finally laid to rest. How wrong could you be? With her eyes closed, she began to feel gentle tears start to gather and seep beneath her lids, and there wasn't anything she could do about it.

He held her away from him briefly. 'Candida?' His voice was soft, enquiring and full of concern, and she looked up at him then, the expression of pain on her face clearly discernible. 'Does it hurt that much?' he murmured.

She shook her head quickly. 'No—no, of course not. It's all right, it's just…' Her lips were trembling with emotion and she couldn't go on.

'What? *What*, then?' he urged. He was still holding her close, so that their bodies melded almost as one.

Candida took a deep breath and gathered herself together, almost shaking him off as she moved away from him. 'This…this won't do, Max,' she said, trying to keep her voice firm. 'I can't—I mustn't…I made up my mind a long time ago that I must never fall into the same trap again, and you're not helping!'

An exasperated sound escaped his lips, and she knew he was annoyed with her. 'Why can't you? What *is* it?' he said, then, almost sullenly, '*Why* are you keeping me away?'

She didn't want him to go on, and said, rather stupidly, 'Just *because*, Max.' Then, 'There's something—there are things you don't know about me…things I can't explain…'

'Well, those are the things I'm hoping to find out,' he said brusquely. 'If I'm ever to be given the chance! Of course there are things I don't know about you— there are things you don't know about *me*!' he added. 'But the first step is to trust each other, and our natural instincts.'

He pulled her towards him again, and she saw a streak of her own blood on his hands. In spite of everything, she rested against him, a huge feeling of despondency sweeping over her. At that moment, much as she wanted it, they could never be anything to each other, she thought. Because she was wised-up now—about worldly men and their fickle desires One dose of the kind of humiliation she'd already suffered was enough for her! Max personified everything that she feared most in a man. Far too handsome for his own good, which ensured him a ready queue of acquiescent females whom he'd have no conscience dumping when they ceased to please him, wealthy, successful, famous… what chance did a serious relationship stand in the face of such significant influences?

And there was that other matter, which Candida could not just dismiss from her mind, as if time had wiped it all out. Because time had *not* wiped it out. It had not done its reputed healing. How could it? She'd been so young, so tender, so full of hope—hope which he, this man who was holding her so tightly, had dashed. Just imagine, she thought, if she did decide to let him get close, really close—could she keep quiet about that impact on her life for ever? Just never refer to it? Never tell him how their paths had once so fleetingly crossed? The fact was, she told herself honestly, she knew she didn't have the *guts* to talk to him about it…simply because she could not bear the prospect of being embarrassed a second time! He would almost certainly remember her book perfectly well, and would have no hesitation in lambasting it all over again! That was too horrible to contemplate! No—she could never expose herself to that possibility, she thought, briefly ashamed again at her lack of courage.

But—what had he just said? That they should trust each other? Well, didn't trust start with no secrets in the background? she asked herself, realising with a kind of helplessness that this relationship had been doomed from the start. However much she thought that she wanted him, he could never be the man for her. Quite apart from the fact that *he'd* stated all too clearly that he never intended to commit himself to any woman, marriage to a writer had little chance of survival. He couldn't have stated his own position more clearly than that!

Candida moved away, stooping to pick up the bags of fruit and wiping her cheek with the back of her hand—making her face more of a mess than ever.

'I didn't even bring a tissue with me,' she said shakily.

'No, and I've got nothing suitable, either,' he said flatly. 'Come on—let's get you and the blasted black-

berries back to the car. We'll stop at the nearest place
to get you cleaned up.'

He took her firmly by the hand and Candida was
glad of the support, because she was feeling totally
drained—not by the scratches she'd sustained, but by
how her life seemed to have so quickly changed from a
rather uneventful norm to one filled with impon-
derables. Why had she ever let him enter her life? Why
had she let him get close? He'd managed to seduce
her—not in the normally accepted sense, that much she
had avoided—but to seduce her emotionally. It was time
to draw a line, she thought desperately.

As he strode effortlessly along beside her, helping her
over the rougher patches now and then, Max's thoughts
were in a muddle all of their own. Why was this woman
getting to him like this? Why couldn't he just have a bit
of fun with her, like he normally did with new females?
What was he getting so hung up about? Hadn't he
promised himself a life free of serious relationships?

But that was what he wanted with Candida, and he
couldn't deny it. Because he liked her. Liked her enough
to want to really get to know her. It was difficult for him
to work it out, but he felt a kinship with her—felt a kind
of meeting of souls which he'd never felt before with
any other female. Max licked his lips quickly. His mouth
had dried, and small beads of perspiration stood out on
his wide forehead. Why was he in this tangle now, of
all times? He could do without it—but he knew himself
to be caught up in a web of desire and determination to
get his own way.

It took a long time going back because now it was
all up hill, but eventually they reached the car, and

Candida thankfully got in, immediately pulling down the vanity mirror to see the damage. She gasped instinctively at her reflection. She was looking a complete mess, with strands of her hair stuck firmly to the streaks of dirt and dried blood all down one side of her face. She reached into her holdall for a tissue, realising that she'd forgotten to bring any make-up with her. Anyway, she thought, shrugging to herself, I need a wash, not camouflage!

Max had been pouring more water for the dog, and now he peered in at her through the open window. 'We'll get somewhere as soon as we can to sort you out.' He paused. 'Bloody hell, Candida, I hope those wounds don't feel as horrible as they look...are you feeling OK?' His voice and expression were full of concern, and Candida looked across at him quickly.

'It's my pride that's pinching the most,' she said. 'If I hadn't been so greedy I'd have left that last little bunch of blackberries where they were and then I wouldn't be in this state.' She looked at her reflection again, and grinned. 'Whatever do I look like?'

Max paused for a second as he stood there looking at her. 'You look...fine...Candida,' he murmured. 'It'll take more than a little tumble to spoil you.' And it was true, he thought. Somehow, looking slightly dirty and dishevelled, with her once immaculate shirt appearing less than perfect, Candida had a childish vulnerability which he found just as appealing as when he'd first seen her, looking like a model at his sister's party.

Almost at once they set off on the homeward journey—Candida preferring to go straight back to her flat, rather than stop en route. 'I've stopped bleeding,' she said, 'so there's no point in delaying further. I just don't feel like facing anyone in this state.'

'OK—fine,' he said coolly, and Candida thought that he'd probably hoped to extend the day until much later—possibly with yet another meal thrown in. It was still only seven o'clock.

She turned to glance out of the window as they drove along rapidly. Somehow she *must* cool this relationship before it went any further—and being in the man's company was not the way to do it! The more they were together, the more impossible it was... Surely the only important thing now was to stick to their business arrangement and provide the necessary service at his apartment—then get out of his life, fast!

He seemed to be reading her thoughts, because presently he said, 'When can I expect to see those samples you're arranging to bring over? The sooner it's all sorted, the better. I've got an infernally busy schedule over the next six weeks or so, and thinking of anything other than the book trade will be difficult.'

'I'm picking them up next week,' Candida replied. 'Tell me any day you're free, and I'll fit in.' She frowned to herself. She only had one contract on-going at the moment, plus two enquiries to follow up. She'd not known work to be this slow for a long time. Then she reassured herself—Christmas was less than three months away, and people always seemed to want makeovers or things done in time for the festive season. In a month or so her phone wouldn't stop ringing, she told herself hopefully. Then she'd be run off her feet!

'I'm free on Wednesday,' he said abruptly, not looking at her. 'After lunch. Not before.'

Candida glanced across at him, at the stern profile, the uncompromising mouth and chin. He'd been very quiet as they'd driven along, obviously deep in thought. She would love to know what was going on in that elegant head, what lay behind his expression.. She sighed inwardly. She wished they hadn't gone blackberrying, because somehow her little accident had changed things…had changed the course of an otherwise perfect day. And it seemed to her it had changed his attitude. From relaxed and carefree to sombre and inward-looking. She hoped that when they reached home he'd go straight away. All she wanted to do was have a warm bath and put some soothing balm on her wounds. Looking down at the backs of her hands again, she grimaced.

At last he drew up outside her flat, and, switching off the engine, turned to look at her.

'Well, thank you for a brilliant day,' he said, rather formally. 'Brilliant, that is, until you decided that we should go blackberrying. Not that I shan't enjoy the tarts you've promised to make me,' he added, 'but they'll come at some cost, won't they?' He gazed down, wincing slightly as his glance fell on Candida's hands and arms.

She looked back at him ruefully. 'All my own fault,' she said lightly. 'But I mend pretty quickly. Usually.' She paused. 'And thank *you* for a super day—one which I didn't expect. And the unexpected things are always the best, I find.'

As soon as she'd made that remark Candida wished she hadn't, because the thing which was uppermost in her mind—and which wouldn't be far from *his*—was how he had demonstrated his feelings for her. *That* had been the most unexpected part of the occasion, she thought, and even though she didn't want it to, she knew that it had surpassed the glorious weather, the idyllic countryside, and the amazing meal they'd enjoyed. But she had somehow succeeded in making him realise— or she hoped she had—that she wanted that side of things to go no further.

Looking up at him again, and meeting the dark softness of his murderously seductive eyes, she felt her heart flutter erratically. Why had they *ever* met up? she asked herself. In another world, under other circum-stances, he could have been the man of her dreams.

Now, saying no more, but obviously with thoughts of his own, he shrugged slightly, then got out of the car and came around to her side, opening the door. After turning briefly to smooth the dog goodbye, Candida picked up her holdall and got out.

'Ella didn't even open one eye to wish me farewell,' she said, smiling up at Max.

'Oh, well, it's been a long day. She's shattered now,' he replied. 'After her supper she'll snore until morning.'

Then, without even a peck on Candida's cheek, he went around to the other side of the car and opened the door. 'Until Wednesday, then?' he said casually.

'Wednesday,' she agreed. '*After* lunch!'

Then he watched her unlock her door and disappear from sight, before driving away rapidly into the advancing twilight.

Upstairs, Candida couldn't wait to begin the cleaning-up process on her face and hands, but suddenly the telephone started to ring. Frowning, she went into the sitting room and picked up the receiver. When she heard the voice at the other end, she nearly dropped the instrument in amazement! What did *he* want? she asked herself angrily?

'Hi…Candy…it's me, darling. How are you?' There was a pause. 'How're you doing?'

Candida's hackles rose nearly to screaming point, but she managed to control her voice as she answered.

'Oh, it's you, Grant,' she said coldly. Well, go on, then, she thought. What is this all about?

'Just wondering how you were—how life's treating you,' the man went on, unperturbed. 'I've missed you.' he added softly.

Oh, really? Candida thought witheringly. This man was impossible! He'd done this once before, after they'd split. Had found himself at a loose end on a Saturday night and tried to re-establish their relationship! But she'd given him a piece of her mind on that occasion, and he'd better pin back his ears for another broadside! Hadn't he got the message the first time?

'Well, well,' she said, injecting a deliberate note of heavy sarcasm into her voice 'How—touching—it is when one is missed! But—sorry to be blunt, Grant—I haven't missed *you* one bit! Not a single tiddly-squat! You are—how can I put this delicately?—you are a "yesterday" man. Old news, Grant. The sort you wrap your fish and chip supper in and then chuck!' she added.

There was a light chuckle at the other end. 'You always were slick with words, Candy,' he said. 'Never left anyone in any doubt as to what you *really* thought!' There was a pause. 'But ever heard the phrase "forgiving and forgetting"?' he suggested. 'It was…good… wasn't it, what we had?'

Candida was furious. How *dared* he have the nerve

to contact her—after all this time? He'd played her—and at least two other women that *she* knew about—like pathetic fish on a hook! He had no shame, no conscience—and he was at it again!

Her cheeks flamed with annoyance.

'Get lost, Grant,' she said sweetly, in a deliberately bored tone. 'Do me the only favour I'm ever likely to ask of you. Get lost!'

And with that Candida slammed down the phone and marched back into the bathroom.

Staring into the mirror, she stopped dabbing at her scratched skin for a second, and looked into her own eyes in the mirror. What was she reading in the expression she saw there? Had Grant been sent by her guardian angel as a warning to her? she wondered. Grant and Max. Max and Grant. Two of a kind? Grant had made himself so special to her, and there had been the distinct possibility that Max was capable of doing the same thing! What was the *matter* with her? But I'm only human, she wined to herself pathetically. And when he had taken her into his arms, when they'd lain together on that soft, grassy bank, nature had almost taken over, lost her again to the soft, intimate touch of a desirable male. Because although she had not let it go any further, that was not the same thing as not *wanting* it to go further!

Angry with herself, Candida filled the handbasin with tepid water and reached for some more cotton wool. Well, she *did* have something to thank wretched Grant for, after all. For reminding her, for strengthening her resolve not to fall for yet another callous, self-centred heart-throb. Grow up, she said to herself through gritted teeth. *Grow up!*

CHAPTER EIGHT

GLANCING through her diary at nine o'clock the following Wednesday morning, Candida frowned briefly. A new client—a neighbour down the road—had just rung to see if Candida could make her professional visit rather later that morning than they'd arranged—which would mean that her appointment at Max's apartment would have to be at four instead of two-thirty, as they'd planned. Candida chewed the top of her pencil. She didn't think that it would make that much difference to Max, but she'd better ring his secretary now, she thought, to make sure she wouldn't be inconveniencing him.

Dialling his number, she waited, expecting to hear Janet's voice, but instead it was another woman who spoke, and at once Candida froze to the spot. Fiona! What was *she* doing there so early in the morning? But why ask? she thought derisively.

'Oh—hello,' Candida faltered. 'Janet?'

'No, Janet's not here today,' the woman replied. 'Can I help you?'

'Um, it's Candida Greenway—' the girl began, and she was interrupted.

'Ah, yes—Max told me you were paying a visit this afternoon.'

'Is he there?' Candida asked, feeling as if she'd been hit in the stomach. The woman had obviously spent the night at the apartment, which could only mean one thing!

'No, 'fraid not. He's out with the dog,' Fiona replied, yawning loudly. 'Oh, dear, excuse me…a *very* late night!' she added meaningfully. 'He'll be back in an hour, I expect, because he'll be wanting his breakfast! Can I give him a message for you?'

'Yes, please,' Candida said, swallowing hard and trying to be reasonable. What business was it of hers who Max Seymour shared his bed with? 'Just say that I can't be there until a bit later than we agreed this afternoon—around four o'clock.'

'No problem. I'm sure he won't mind,' Fiona said possessively, as if she was privy to everything going on in Max's life and could speak for the man.

'Well, thanks,' Candida said lamely. 'If you'll just let him know…'

'Of course I will. Goodbye.' And the phone went dead. Candida stood back, squaring her shoulders. Well, that was proof enough, if proof were needed! Proof of Max's superficial attitude to emotional relationships, she thought. To him they were mere passing fancies. *Why* had she thought otherwise? Why had she thought that the way he'd enveloped her in his strong arms might have meant as much to him as it had—at that moment— meant to her? Candida's shoulders drooped. Max was just another two-timer. Or ten-timer, probably, in his case! And if she'd been in any doubt as to the direction her life should take, she thought decisively, she was in doubt no longer! All the messages were coming through loud and clear!

Later on that day Candida found herself once more at the mansion apartment, where she'd brought the swatches for Max's approval. She was thankfully aware that Fiona had obviously taken herself off, and without looking at Max as she followed him into the sitting area, she said casually, 'I take it that Fiona gave you my message? That I was to be a bit later than we'd arranged?'

'She did,' he replied solemnly. 'Thank you.'

Then he retreated to his study, while Candida arranged everything for his inspection. Well, whichever he selected would look fabulous, she thought. The height and breadth of the windows and the vast floor area had given plenty of scope for her artistic imagination to indulge itself. How she would love, she thought, to be choosing this for herself!

She sat on the floor in the sunshine for a minute or two, with Ella stretched out contentedly beside her, and she couldn't help thinking again what a lucky animal she was to have Max as her owner. He gave the dog every consideration, not just because he should, but because he clearly adored her. That was one up to him!

Presently, he came out of his study and across to the window. By the pensive look on his face Candida could see that he was still totally preoccupied with what he'd been doing, and she made a face to herself. He didn't even glance at the carpet samples on the floor, but stood gazing down at the scene below them, his hands thrust in his pockets. Ah, Candida thought, this was Maximus

Seymour the great author! This was not the man who'd held her to him in that brief moment of passion—and by the look of it even the Fiona effect must have worn off pretty quickly, too! With a huge effort she pushed these thoughts from her mind. Now it was business. For both of them!

She looked up at him with an enquiring glance. 'I thought you might like to consider one of these three shades for this room, Max, for the flooring. And any of these drapes would look good…' She picked up one of the small swatches of fabric, and held it against the window. 'See…? I could envisage those complementing each other, or…' She paused and took up another swatch. 'This is a favourite with several of my clients, and would look absolutely perfect in this room…'

He hadn't said a word as Candida had been explaining, but suddenly he said, 'Yeah—any of those'll do.' He stared down at her. 'You choose, Candida—you choose what you'd like for yourself.'

'Pardon?' Candida was momentarily taken aback, though after a second's thought wasn't surprised. She'd seen as soon as they'd met that afternoon that his mind was anywhere but there—that having to make decisions about unimportant details concerning fabrics and furnishings for his home was the last thing he was going to concern himself with.

She hesitated. 'Max,' she began patiently, 'my choice is not necessarily going to agree with yours. It really is always a matter of personal taste in the end, and—'

'Yes, well, make it a matter of *your* personal taste,' he said shortly. 'After all, you're the one with the know-how, and that's what you did for Faith—she left it all to

you, didn't she? And look how that turned out. No…'
He stared out of the window again. 'I'm happy to entrust
you with bringing my home up to a more contemporary
style and standard, and don't worry. That was what I'd
always intended. I haven't got the time to put any
thought to it—especially at the moment, with another
deadline in November.'

He ran his hand restlessly through his hair, and
Candida realised that everything he was saying was
true. His heart and mind were very definitely elsewhere.
She might just as well do as she was told and enjoy
herself selecting the items she would love to have in the
place if it was hers—and all at his expense!

She glanced up at him quickly, and shrugged. 'Well,
if you're happy with that arrangement,' she said, 'what
can I say? Except that it will probably prove to be an
expensive enterprise!'

He said nothing to that, but was plainly relieved that
he wasn't going to have to waste time on what he saw
as something incidental to his important life. 'Thanks,'
he said, turning to go back into his study, and for the first
time that day he smiled his disarming smile. But for
once Candida was able to dismiss it with indifference.

Presently, preparing to leave, Candida began gathering everything together, thinking that at least she could
make this particular contract a speedy one—not having
to wait for Max's approval or otherwise would be a
great help! She'd been given a free hand to order
whatever she wanted—so she'd get on with it! And *then*,
hopefully, wave Max Seymour a final goodbye!

Emerging from his study again, he said casually, 'I'm
going to make some tea—will you join me?'

'No—sorry…I can't stay…things to do,' Candida said firmly. 'I've got some stuff to prepare for the morning, and—'

'But it's only five o'clock,' he interrupted. 'There's plenty of day left, surely?'

'No—I do need to get back…'

'Please stay, Candida,' he said, and Candida realised that this was a plea—not a command—a plea for her company. She felt it with all her sensitive intuitiveness. Despite not feeling particularly well-disposed towards him at the moment, she knew she probably would agree to his request. 'Please….?' he added, looking down at her, and she couldn't help noticing how tired and drawn he appeared. Well, he should go to bed earlier, she thought. And sometimes, preferably, by himself!

She bit her lip. He seemed terribly uptight about his book launch, and at this moment in time for some reason he wanted company. Well, she was here, and she might as well stay—at least for a little while. If it meant that much to him to have someone share a pot of tea and talk for a bit—she'd oblige. She was used to having to please clients!

'All right—just for half an hour, then,' she said. Putting down her things, she followed him into the kitchen, and watched while he filled the kettle.

He held her gaze for a moment or two, then said suddenly, 'I wonder…I wonder if you'd do me a really big favour, Candida….?'

Candida looked away. Probably not! she thought.

'I've had an idea, and I reckon you could be the answer to one of my many problems,' he said.

Candida immediately felt a warning tingle in her veins. 'What exactly are you talking about?' she asked, her mind running in ten directions at once as she tried to imagine what he was going to ask of her—and tried to have as many objections ready as to fit the case!

'Well, quite apart from everything else going on at the moment,' he said slowly, 'I've just been reminded by my agent that I've got a prestigious short story competition coming up…. I'm the final judge, in this one, and there'll be about a dozen to choose from. They'll all be good. One winner and two runners-up, with considerable cash prizes.'

Candida looked at him, her eyebrows raised. 'So?' she said. 'What can *I* do about it?'

'You can read through them as well and give me your opinion.' He paused. 'Judging other people's work is a massive responsibility—and I hate doing it. I'm always afraid of getting it wrong.'

Candida's face flushed crimson at these words, all those feelings of hers which she thought she had well under control springing to life again. So…he hated judging did he? That was news to her! He'd seemed to relish every single word when he'd judged *her*! And now he was asking her to help him judge others…what a turnaround in the order of things! Was she *dreaming*? And how could she possibly agree to do it? How could she possibly agree to this—perhaps be at least partly responsible for disappointing or even destroying someone else's hopes and aspirations? She shook herself inwardly. Surely this was a step too far—a step she was not going to take!

She cleared her throat. 'Why on earth do you think that *I'd* be a good judge of any writer's work?' she asked bluntly. 'How can I possibly be worthy of the task?'

'I think you'd be perfect at it,' he said at once. 'You are imaginative, intuitive, you think deeply about things… Of course, the more technical aspects of short story-writing may not come within your scope, but I can deal with all those minor details. No…I'd like your natural, sensitive response as to what makes a story special, what makes it stand out, what makes it stay in the memory. What it does for *you*, it would do for any intelligent reader. And that would be the one that wins.'

Candida felt almost overwhelmed. How could *she*, an unpublished author, possibly be thought up to judging anyone else? That her opinion could perhaps sway Max's professional assessment of a manuscript was too much of a burden. She just could not do it!

'I think you're asking the wrong person, Max,' she said, trying to keep her voice light. 'You should ask another writer…'

'But I am,' he replied coolly, looking down at her. 'I think I see you as a potential author, Candida. They say it takes one to know one—well, I'm beginning to know you rather well. I understand your feelings, your response to things…even the way you commented on my books convinced me of it straight away.' He thought for a moment. 'You've never actually said whether you'd ever done any writing yourself, but I'd be surprised if you hadn't at some time…'

Candida stared up at him—was this yet another chance to tell all? she asked herself. But once again she let the moment pass.

'Oh, I dabbled—like every other person who could hold a pencil,' Candida replied casually. 'The only evidence was my winning the school literary prize two years running, but…'

'Ah, I was right, then,' he said. He searched her face, and it seemed to Candida that he was penetrating her very soul. 'I believe you could be a writer yourself one day—if you wanted to, that is. I don't doubt that you could commit to the task, and I believe you could be successful. Very successful.'

Candida stood right away from him, but refused to unlock her gaze from his. What had she ever done to be in this position? she asked herself. To have and have not, seemed to fit the case! So—Maximus Seymour thought she could be a successful writer, did he? Huh! she thought witheringly, as his words finally sank in. That was *not* your previous opinion, so publicly aired, Mr Wonderful Author, as you looked down from your lofty height! Those were *not* the words you used when you threw all that cold water over my poor, unsophisticated head!

They stood there in a silence ruffled only by the humming of the kettle as it began to boil, and Candida looked away, her thoughts running riot. She wouldn't do this thing he'd asked of her, she thought instinctively. She didn't feel capable of it. And she'd use work as her excuse. He'd have to get on with this by himself.

'I'll have to think about…your request,' she said. 'It rather depends on my own work-load. I'll let you know.'

'Well, there's not much time,' he said flatly, reaching for the box of tea. 'It's the middle of October now, and they want my final decision by the thirty-first. And of course, there's the other small matter of my book launch….' His brows knitted in a dark frown as he thought about that. 'Anyway,' he said, 'I'll have all the submissions here by the weekend, so that gives us two weeks.'

Gives *us* two weeks? Candida thought. Gives *you* two weeks, Max, not me! He was automatically assuming that she was going to agree—yet even as his annoying assumption was getting to her she couldn't deny that she was feeling a surge of gratification that he thought her opinion could help him make the right decision, would actually help him find the winner of this competition. And, if she was honest, she would love to do it! To sit back and enjoy, wallow in twelve or more brilliant stories… He'd said that he was the final judge, so they would already have been pored over and sifted by others, and would obviously be exceptional entries—it would hardly be a chore! It would be a privilege—a pleasure! The only disadvantage being that she would want everyone to win! To think of discarding all the other fantastic ones in order to find the best would cut her to the quick!

Just then the buzzer to the entrance door sounded, and Max frowned. 'Hmm,' he murmured, 'I'm not expecting callers today.'

With Ella trotting curiously ahead of him, he left Candida standing there and went out across the hall—immediately she heard a babble of excited voices as Max opened the door and greeted his visitors.

'Wow! What are *you* doing here!' he said, the warm delight in his voice matching little Emily's excited chatter.

Candida smiled. Fantastic—it could only be Faith and her little daughter!

She was right, and straight away they all came into the kitchen to join her, Emily held closely in Max's arms. Faith automatically went across to Candida and hugged her affectionately.

'Candida!' the woman exclaimed. 'I had no *idea* we'd be seeing you today as well! What a treat!' She bent to pat the dog. 'Oh, Ella! Good girl! Yes, I know—we're pleased to see you, too!' Then she studied Candida's appearance for a second: 'Oh, dear—what did you do to your face?' she enquired. 'That's been painful.'

Candida pursed her lips ruefully—even while fleetingly realising that Max hadn't even bothered to mention her skirmish with the blackberry bush, or enquire as to how her wounds were healing. 'Oh, it's nothing really, Faith,' she said, avoiding Max's gaze. 'I caught myself on a thorn, that's all. It's much better— and thank goodness for make-up!'

Now she *did* look across at Max, who she sensed had been staring at her, his expression serious. She wondered if he'd given the slightest thought to their picnic and, much, much more vitally—remembered how he'd kissed her so passionately. Despite all her good intentions, *she'd* certainly remembered it! But of *course* it hadn't meant anything at all to him, she thought, almost savagely. She was just one in a long line! She turned away from him quickly, before his perceptive mind could interpret her present thoughts and conflict. Because sometimes she felt that he was actually right there inside her head…and her heart.

Max, too, was aware of the fact that they hadn't made any physical contact today—not even touched or brushed past each other. For their own reasons, they had kept their distance. When she'd arrived at the door earlier he'd had the utmost difficulty not to gather her to him, to feel her soft body in his arms and smother her face with kisses. But he knew that if he had he'd have killed their relationship—such as it was—for ever. After momentarily succumbing to his advances the other day, she'd pushed him away, rejected him—and he had no idea how he was going to get past her objections. His only possible hope lay in treading very, very carefully, while somehow finding reasons for them to be together.

Candida realised that while she'd been deep in thought Faith had been talking animatedly about their morning in town, and now the woman went on, 'It seems ages ago that we were together, Candida. Emmy often asks me when you're coming back to the cottage.'

The child held out her arms to Candida, who immediately took her from Max to cuddle her.

'Hey, she's *my* little favourite, not yours!' he said teasingly. 'Give her back at once!'

'In a minute—when I've had my turn,' Candida said firmly.

Faith threw her bag down onto one of the basket weave chairs and went over to the window. 'Oh, look— this view is just wonderful! We don't come here often enough, do we, Emmy?' She turned around to look up at Max. 'We were in your neck of the woods today, brother dearest,' she said lightly. 'We had lunch with Rick first, and then thought we couldn't go home without coming to see you as well—as we were so close. Good job you were at home!' She looked pointedly at the things Max had begun to put out. 'And anyway, I'm parched, so we're staying to tea.'

'It's brilliant to see you, Faith,' Max said, and Candida was quietly surprised at how Max's mood had changed in an instant—as if by magic. He must adore his family, she thought—and why not? Faith, as pretty and effervescent as ever, seemed to glow with a kind of happy well-being that was infectious. And Candida felt the warmth of it herself as they stood there in a little circle, with Emily looking so sweet in her fashionable little girl's outfit.

Max reached for two more mugs from the shelf. 'If you'd only rung first I'd have got in some cakes from the deli…' he said.

'Oh, I knew there'd be nothing worth eating *here*,' Faith said cheerfully. 'So I've brought a box of pastries with me.' She opened her shopping bag and handed it to Max, then turned to Candida. 'I only heard recently about Max asking you to help him update things here a bit, Candida,' she said. 'Which I must tell you is a surprise, because he's terrible at making up his mind about anything domestic. I have to nag him every now and then if I think he's neglecting things.' She smiled up at her brother. 'And I'm afraid I do have grave doubts about his required intake of daily portions of fruit and veg!'

Candida smiled as she listened to Faith's good-natured chat about her brother, trying not to catch Max's eye. She supposed it was like this with all famous people, she thought. Outside the boundaries of their outward success they were just normal—part of a normal family, with all the same petty preoccupations as everyone else. But she didn't think that Faith should worry about Max's diet—even if it was catered for mainly by expensive food from high-class restaurants and delis! Because he was well-built, with a lean and powerful frame which exhibited taut, well-toned muscles. Candida could just imagine the distance he and the dog would cover most days on their walks.

Emily asked to be put down, then, and toddled over to where Ella was lying full-stretch on the floor, her tail thumping gently as the child curled up beside her.

Candida went across and opened the box which Faith had brought with her, placing the cakes on a large plate she selected from the side unit. 'These look lovely, Faith,' she said, and the woman's eyes twinkled, her quick mind taking in the small, familiar move which Candida had just made. It proved one thing to her…Candida was no stranger here and knew her way around Max's kitchen! Wouldn't it be *wonderful*, Faith thought, if Max and Candida could be a couple? From the very first, she'd hoped that the girl might appeal to her brother, because the big thing missing from his life was a strong relationship with someone he could love and trust, be comfortable with at last.

Presently, they all sat up together at the long kitchen bar to have their tea, and Emily came over to lean comfortably against Max's knees as she nibbled at her cake. He looked down at her, his eyes warm and soft, his hand caressing the top of the curly head.

'Pity it's not someone's birthday,' he murmured, 'then we could have had some candles to blow out, because this feels like a party to me,' he added playfully.

Just then, the phone rang, and he left the room to answer it. Candida smiled across at Faith.

'I'm really glad you called in, Faith,' she said. 'Max seems a different person when you and Emily are around.' She paused. 'I imagine that he relies very heavily on you—on you and Rick.'

'Oh, no, that's not really the case,' Faith said at once. 'My brother is—well—he's just very special. He's always there when we need him, but he never pushes himself. He can't bear to feel he's intruding on us, on our family, but we both tell him that he's always, always welcome—and always will be at our home.' She looked away for a second, lowering her voice. 'A few years ago Rick went through a terrible patch. He wasn't very well at the time, there was a lot going on at work, and he had to make several people—some of them friends—redundant. It nearly gave him a nervous breakdown.'

She drank from her mug of tea, and her eyes looked troubled at the memory. 'If it hadn't been for Max I don't think he'd have come through it at all. But Max was a confidante, a rock, a tower of strength. He had just the way of talking to Rick, and making him see the bigger picture. Of course Max couldn't alter anything, or make the problems disappear, but he gave Rick the time to talk and talk…they talked for hours at a time! Naturally, I was often there too, but it's different for two men to discuss things, and Max was just that little distance away emotionally so that he could be more objective about everything.'

She paused for a long moment. 'We'll always be very grateful for my brother's support at that time. Though I know he can be a very complex being,' she added brightly. 'Especially when a new book is about to hit the shelves! I try to be around as much as possible to take his mind off things a bit, because he does get very uptight—and moody, I'm afraid.'

Candida nodded. 'Yes, I've seen that over the last week or so,' she said slowly, privately thinking that he *did* have the ability to switch off when it suited him! 'But I find it hard to understand,' she went on, 'what Max has to fear, with all his success behind him. And he's always had the huge advantage of your mother's influence, hasn't he?'

Faith waited a few moments before speaking, then shook her head. 'No, Max and my mother were never that close. There was a sort of tension between them. Of course Maxy is a proud man—he was much too proud to refer to her if he had a problem. He always had to do his own thing.' She sighed. 'And Dad was so tolerant—of both of them. So sweet and gentle.'

Thinking about it, as she listened to what Faith was saying, Candida wasn't surprised. Yes, Max was undoubtedly a proud man, she thought. She was beginning to think of him as that, rather than an arrogant monster, and she could readily believe that he wouldn't have expected any favours from his famous mother.

Faith bent down to wipe some sugar from Emily's lips. 'I don't think you should have another cake, darling,' she said, as the little girl went to help herself from the plate. 'Or you might be sick on the way home!'

Max came in then, and gathered Emily up into his arms again, holding her close to him. He looked down at Candida. 'The competition stories will be delivered by hand tomorrow—a few days earlier than expected,' he said. 'They've just let me know.'

Candida returned his gaze steadily, opening her mouth to say something, but he went on quickly, 'So—between us I think we'll have enough time to sort it, don't you?' He looked over to Faith. 'I've asked Candida to help me with the competition stories,' he explained, and Faith cut in.

'Oh—I forgot you told me you had that to do as well, Maxy! I don't call that good planning—maybe you should sack your agent!' She turned to Candida. 'That is so good of you, Candida—to spare some of your time for Max. I'm sure you've got plenty on your own plate! And talking of which, I'm not going to ask you a single thing about what you're going to be doing for him in this place. I shall wait until it's all done, and then come and admire it!'

The woman's excitement and pleasure at recognising what she saw as the obvious development in Max and Candida's association was patently clear—and Candida felt somewhat trapped. How could she be stand-offish and throw cold water on the situation? He'd cornered her in the way that was becoming all too familiar, and although part of her resented it, a far larger part of her relished it! How could she *not* enjoy being with this family? she thought. It wouldn't be for ever, after all, so she might just as well enjoy the present. The past had taken care of itself so far, and would go on doing so. In any case, the judging of these stories might prove to be the watershed—the final moment of revelation when she would find the nerve, at last, to tell Max Seymour just what he'd done to her.

Suddenly Faith's mobile rang. Answering it, she said, 'Hi, darling.' She glanced across at the others. 'It's Rick,' she said. Then, 'Yes, we'll be on our way now.' She looked at her watch. 'Meet you in…forty-five minutes, where we said. OK.' She switched off the phone and smiled. 'Rick's leaving work early so we can all go home together,' she said happily.

'Let me drop you somewhere—' Max began, but Faith interrupted.

'Don't be silly, Maxy. The tube's at the end of your road, and I've got our tickets. No need for you to drive me.' She picked up her things. 'Well, it may not have been anyone's birthday,' she said, 'but it felt like a family party to me, too!'

Candida smiled. 'Talking of birthdays, we've got an important date coming up in our family—well, in my little family, I should say.' She added. 'My father is going to be sixty on the second of December, so a couple of his pals and I are organising a surprise party for him.'

'How lovely!' Faith said, 'Are there good places for functions in the area, Candida?'

'Oh, yes—I suppose so,' Candida replied. 'But my dad wouldn't like anything too posh! No, it's going to be held in the village hall, and the choir he belongs to will put on some entertainment…they'll sing, and there'll be local instrumentalists. And there's going to be a bit of a barn dance.' She paused. 'The problem will be keeping it all a secret from him—but they've promised me they'll manage it somehow. Dad thinks it's just going to be me and him, and two of his best friends..' She paused. 'I'll arrange the catering with local ladies, of course—that's what'll appeal to Dad. He's not into the high life!'

'Well, it's his day, so he must have what he wants, mustn't he?' Faith said. She paused. 'I think that sounds lovely, Candida—like a Thomas Hardy novel. Unsophisticated, and thoroughly enjoyable.' She glanced at her brother. 'We've always celebrated things in hotels and restaurants, haven't we, Maxy? Nothing so imaginative as what you're going to be doing, Candida.'

Max looked across at Candida. 'And will there be…cawl…on the menu?' he murmured, and she smiled up at him.

'Oh, no, not in the evening. But we'll have some for our lunch, I expect.'

'What on earth is cawl?' Faith wanted to know.

'Cawl,' Max said, slowly and deliberately, as if about to explain something of national importance, 'is a Welsh stew, made with Welsh lamb, simmered slowly, and preferably done the day before eating so that any extraneous fat may be skimmed off, with onions, potatoes, possibly carrots and parsley—lots—added. Cawl is not thickened, but served very hot, and seasoned generously with salt and pepper.' He didn't look at Candida as he went on. 'The word rhymes with "scowl" and "growl" and "howl", and to my mind sounds threatening and positively dangerous—though Candida assures me that it's delicious. Nourishing and warming.'

Candida couldn't help laughing—realising that not only had he remembered everything she'd said about it, but had almost certainly looked it up somewhere—because *she* hadn't gone into such detail. And looking up at him, at the amusement in those tantalising blue-black eyes, she shook her head briefly. *What* was she to do with this man? she asked herself. How was she to rid herself of him? She knew she could do it physically—but emotionally? Then, with a cold shiver, her thoughts returned to the woman he'd just spent the night with….not very far away from where they were standing! *That* was enough to keep her grounded!

'I think it sounds very appetising,' Faith said. 'Come to Farmhouse Cottage and make some for all of us to enjoy, Candida. My butcher will get me Welsh lamb if I ask for it,' she added.

Faith prepared to leave with Emily, then, and they all went towards the door. She gave Candida a hug. 'Thank you, Candida—for everything,' she added significantly. 'I'll give you a ring tomorrow, and we'll make a date for us all to be together at the cottage.'

Max crouched down to hug Emily, saying something in her ear as the child giggled excitedly, and Faith said, out of the corner of her mouth to Candida, 'Keep the last weekend in the month free.' She knew that of course that would be crunch time for Max's new novel.

Faith glanced at her brother as he stood up again. 'Maxy, you need to be away from this place and out in the open air,' she said. She patted his arm. 'You're looking drawn. Have an early night now and then, for goodness' sake!'

Max grinned down at his sister good naturedly. 'You worry about me too much, Faith.'

She cut in, 'Well, if *I* don't, who will?' she demanded.

'Actually, last night *was* rather exceptional,' he went on casually, leaning against the doorframe for a minute. 'In fact, we didn't get any sleep until about five a.m.'

'Five a.m.?' Faith echoed. 'What on earth were you doing up at that time?'

Candida almost shrivelled up inside! She did not want to hear the rest of this—did not want to be part of this discussion! She hoped Max wasn't going to give a blow-by-blow account of his night of unbridled passion with Fiona whatever-her-name-was!

'Well, you see, I'd had a long, long, meeting all day at my agent's. It went on until after ten, and we were just about done when I got a phone call from Rob Winters...'

'Oh, yes, Rob—you were best man at his wedding about two years or so ago, weren't you?'

'Well remembered, Faith,' Max said, smiling, and Faith turned to Candida.

'Rob and Max go way back, to boarding school days,' she explained.

'We've not spoken for a while,' Max went on, 'he's abroad quite a bit now—but apparently at teatime yesterday his wife presented him with their firstborn—a boy weighing in at nine pounds! I'd known they were expecting a happy event, but wasn't sure when. Anyway, naturally Rob wanted to celebrate, and I was the first person he thought of to celebrate with! So I went straight over to his place following my meeting, and after drinking an inordinate amount of the best champagne we finally crashed out at about five a.m., I believe. I didn't drag myself back here until eight—and then I took the dog for a very long walk to restore my common sense!'

Candida's mind was going all over the place! So he apparently hadn't been here last night—but what on earth had Fiona been doing there so early, apparently making him breakfast?

She looked up quickly—to see Max's eyes barely able to hide their amusement. He'd known very well how she'd sized up—incorrectly—the situation! And he'd enjoyed watching her confusion.

'As it happened,' he continued, turning to Faith, 'Fiona—from my agent's—was in need of a bed for last night. Not only because we were so late finishing, and she lives way out of town, but also because she'd had a call to tell her that the water supply to her flat wouldn't be restored until later today. They've had leakage problems, so she was telling us. So—since I wasn't going to be home—I gave her my key.' He paused, an infuriating smile touching the corners of his mouth. 'All in all, it worked perfectly well for everyone—especially as the Jarretts had Ella for me, solving Fiona's problem with dogs.' He bent to smooth Ella's head as he spoke. 'How could any decent, normal human being object to this wonderful creature?' he murmured. 'Well, we all know what we think of *them*, don't we, Ella?'

Faith and Emily made their departure in a flurry of hugs and kisses and promises, with the little girl having to be distracted from wanting to take the dog with them, and presently Max and Candida were alone again, their unspoken thoughts darting between them like rampant fireflies. He looked down at her.

'I'll spend tomorrow and Friday on those stories,' he said. 'Then you can come over and see them. After that, we'll confer. I know straight away that we'll argue and fight about it—but that's all to the good. However,' he added, 'we will eventually agree. We *must* eventually agree.'

Candida stared up at him, suddenly feeling light-hearted—and light-headed! She hadn't actually *said* she'd help him with his judging—but she didn't have to. Because she knew she was going to. And so did he!

CHAPTER NINE

CANDIDA went into the small bedroom she used as her study, and picked up the telephone. As she dialled Max's mobile, her hand shook slightly. She knew he was not going to be happy—but her mind was finally made up.

It was nine days since she'd seen him—nine days since Faith and Emily had turned up at his apartment—and it was partly that which had brought her to her decision. This had to stop! She must not allow herself to get involved with this family any longer. It was foolish, she thought, and she felt, overwhelmingly, that it could only end badly.

He'd telephoned several times, demanding to know when she'd be joining him to read the stories, and she'd stated—quite truthfully—that her own commitments must come first.

Now, he answered the phone almost immediately, and Candida's knees trembled as she heard those dark, resonant tones, the deep masculinity that throbbed with every word.

'Max? Hi—' she began.

'Ah—at last,' he said, cutting in. 'We've just a few days now before I'm obliged to return these things, so when are you coming over to read them, Candida? I've spent hours going over and over them, and I just cannot make up my mind. I'm really in need of another opinion.'

Candida took a deep breath. 'Well…sorry, Max…but you'll have to ask someone else,' she said, mustering all her courage to be firm and direct. 'I honestly can't see my way to spending time away from my own stuff at the moment.' She swallowed. 'I've got a living to make, and I had another good enquiry yesterday, and if that goes ahead it'll wrap me up for the next couple of months, at least.'

There was a moment's silence, then to Candida's utter amazement she heard a click and the line went dead! She held the instrument away from her in disgust…well, *really*, she thought! He'd hung up on her—actually hung up! She paused for several seconds, not really wanting to believe it. Whatever faults he might have, rudeness and petty, small-mindedness were not among them! Or she'd thought so up until then! He was obviously no gentleman after all, she thought grimly as she replaced the receiver. Then she shrugged. Well, good. That sort of childish behaviour was all she needed to disconnect with him finally. He'd made it easy for her!

She stared disconsolately down at her desk, at the half-completed design she was doing, deciding that what she needed right now was a strong cup of tea. Going out into the kitchen, she'd started to fill the kettle when, without warning, she burst into a flood of tears, releasing the painful lump which had formed in her throat over the last few minutes. Max's behaviour just then had hurt her more deeply than she wanted to confess…even to herself. To have the phone slammed down like that was as bad as a slap in the face!

Trying to make her drink while mopping up the tears which refused to stop wasn't easy, and before she finally carried the tray into her bedroom she'd almost used up a whole box of tissues. Damn and blast Max Seymour, she thought bitterly. Why did he matter so much? Why did she *care* whether she annoyed him or not? And why had his slamming the phone down like that got to her?

Candida knew the answers to her own questions before they were formed. Because she knew he had come to matter to her, and that she would hate to upset him in any way at all. Because she'd come to *like* him, despite her best efforts not to! And by dismissing her as he had he'd made her feel small, hurt and humiliated. Well…was she really surprised? she asked herself. He'd done it before, hadn't he?

She sat on the edge of her bed and sipped at the scalding tea, staring into space for a moment or two. She supposed that that would be the end of her assignment at his apartment—because he was the sort who would take pleasure in being vindictive when his plans were thwarted. He'd just cancel everything. And it would be the end of her association with Faith and Rick and their little daughter, too. But wasn't that what she wanted? What was best for her? Fresh tears threatened to spill down Candida's face again, and she scolded herself for her stupidity. For goodness' *sake*—what was the big deal? She'd only known Faith for about six months—and Max for much less. Her life would hardly grind to a halt without them!

She finished her tea, feeling so dispirited that she lay

down on her bed. Her eyes felt hot and tingly with all the weeping she'd been doing, and it felt really blissful to rest them for a few moments. Perhaps, she thought, it would be good to drop off, have a little sleep…just for a few minutes…

Suddenly, what seemed like only a moment later, her doorbell rang with such urgency that Candida leapt up into a sitting position as if she'd been shot! Who on earth was calling on her? she thought. Glancing at her bedside clock, she saw that it was five-thirty. She must have actually been asleep for an hour and a half!

Swinging her legs over the side of the bed, she caught sight of herself in the mirror opposite, and groaned. Whatever did she look like? Her face was pale and tear-stained, and her hair was a tangly, untidy mess where she'd obviously been tossing and turning. And her white T-shirt was crumpled almost beyond recognition. Well, whoever was outside could go away. She was not seeing visitors today, she thought.

The bell rang again, even more stridently, and, going into the sitting room, she peeped out of the front window to see if she could make out who was standing there.

With a gasp of recognition, she saw Max's Mercedes parked right there across the road! Oh, no! She put her hand to her mouth in horror, realising that he would have noticed her own elderly car parked in its allotted space, and would know that she was probably at home!

When the bell rang for a third time, she knew she had no alternative but to answer it. *And* he'd have to come in…and see her in this state! She lifted her chin defiantly. So *what*? she asked herself. What did any of this matter in the long run? Did she care any more?

Going down the stairs, she opened the front door and stared up at him. For a moment, neither of them spoke. Then she stood aside.

'Would you like to come in?' she asked with studied politeness, as if to emphasise that *she* always treated people with courtesy.

He stepped over the threshold, scrutinising her appearance with overt interest, and Candida cringed. She always took care with how she looked, how she presented herself, but she wasn't up to standard today!

'I thought I was going to have to break the door down,' he said cheerfully. 'Saw your car, so I thought you must be at home.' He paused, not taking his eyes off her. 'Is there something wrong...are you OK, Candida?'

'I'm perfectly OK, thank you,' she said. She turned away to lead him up the stairs. 'Bit of a cold, that's all,' she lied. 'I shouldn't come too close.'

'Oh, I never catch colds—from anyone,' he replied, following her. 'So don't worry about that.'

I'm not worried about you catching anything at all, Candida thought, but I *would* like to know what you're doing here! Uninvited!

They went into the sitting room, and Max placed a large folder on to the coffee table.

'The stories,' he announced. 'Since I realise you're far too busy to come to me, I've come to you instead. There's no reason why we shouldn't confer here, is there?'

He sat down and patted the arm of the chair. 'This is comfortable,' he said amiably

Candida stared down at him, not believing that the man had had the nerve to discount what she'd said about not having the time to read for him. He'd decided to just turn up, unannounced, and more or less force her to do it.

She sighed, and perched on the arm of the chair opposite. 'I don't think you understood what I said on the phone, Max. Even though it turned out to be a somewhat *short* conversation,' she added pointedly.

'Ah, yes—sorry about that. I dropped the damned thing, and didn't think I'd waste time ringing you again,' he said. 'Because we need to do this thing—fast.' He grinned across at her, and Candida forgot her own appearance for a moment. He was *so* good-looking it was infuriating, she thought for the hundredth time. His hair was boyishly untidy around his neck and ears, and his rugged features expressed their usual mix of amusement and cynicism. Then, suddenly, a wave of anger swept over her, and she stood up, going across to the window and turning to face him.

'I don't know what it is with you men,' she said coldly. 'You think the whole world revolves around you and your little schemes. *Your* needs, *your* plans, *your* wishes…they're all that matters, aren't they? Never mind what anyone else wants! I told you that…that I didn't…that I wouldn't…help you with your judging because I have a full diary of my own. But of course that doesn't count, does it, Max? All that counts is Maximus Seymour and his reputation, his grand opinions!'

'Whoa! Hey, what's brought all this on?' he said. He stood up and came over to stand next to her. For an electrifying, terrifying moment Candida thought he was going to take her in his arms…and *that* would have been her undoing!

'I'll tell you what's brought it on,' she flared, determined to stick to her guns. 'First, you're almost forcing me to help you with something that you're perfectly capable of dealing with yourself…and why you should want *my* opinion is still, frankly, beyond me! And you clearly think that your commitments are much more important than any could possibly be in *my* life!'

'I've never said that,' he interrupted. 'And I've certainly never thought it. I admire very much what you do, Candida.'

'But you obviously think that it's not so important that it cannot all be put on hold for *your* requirements!'

He looked down at her, a curious expression on his face. 'I think you're being unreasonable,' he remarked slowly.

'Hah! Unreasonable, am I? Well, perhaps I *am*!' Candida seethed at that remark, remembering, vividly, how Grant had accused her of unreasonableness when she'd sometimes questioned his constant changing of the plans they'd made. It had taken her quite some time to understand—only too well—that the reasons always involved other, more exciting liaisons than theirs!

Max hadn't taken his eyes from her face as she'd spoken, realising that her emotions were in a somewhat heightened state. He wished he could really understand her. Get to the heart of what she felt. What had she meant the other day when'd she'd said there were things he didn't know about her? She was such a patently honest and straightforward woman, he didn't think for a second that she had some dark secret which might have led to court proceedings! And even *that* wouldn't have mattered! He *wanted* this woman! he told himself. And when he got her, she would never feel the need for another man in her life ever again!

To cut the rather intense atmosphere, Max said casually, 'Any chance of a coffee?' and Candida smiled wanly.

'Of course—sorry,' she said quickly, glancing up at him. She brushed past him, going into the kitchen.

He followed, and watched as she started making the drinks. Then he said softly, 'I'm sorry, Candida, if you think I've pushed you into doing something you really didn't want to do.' He paused. 'As a matter of fact, the stories were reasonably easy to sift—and it's only the final five which I'm finding a problem. Not quite knowing in which order to place them. If you…if you could find the time to look at just those and let me know what you think I'd be eternally grateful. And relieved,' he added. 'Judging anything makes me feel like an executioner!'

Candida stopped what she was doing for a moment, poised with the milk bottle in her hand—but decided not to make any comment.

She resumed what she was doing, and they carried the drinks into the sitting room.

'Since it shouldn't take you too long,' Max said, 'I'll wait while you do it, then I can take them back with me.' He drank from his mug. 'The reason that I'm asking this of you, Candida, is because I remember the way you dissected a few of *my* books—everything you said about them struck me as very relevant, salient, and I realised you were able to burrow into a plot, to live it and make a thoughtful assessment of it.'

Candida looked away quickly, but felt ridiculously pleased at his remarks—even if it did show that having to read for him was her own silly fault, after all! She should have kept her big mouth shut!

Much, much later, sitting comfortably in her bed-room while Max watched TV in the sitting room, Candida finally closed the pages of the last story and leaned her head back. She knew exactly which one she'd choose as the winner. To her it was outstanding for its perceptiveness and humour, and Candida wished she'd written it herself!

She rejoined him in the other room and placed the entries on the table. He looked up at her, raising his eyes.

'Number eight,' she said, without preamble. 'Followed by numbers two and eleven. All fantastic stories, I thought, but number eight stood out…had me crying and laughing all at the same time.'

Max stood up and came over to her, an expression of relief on his face. 'Thank heaven for that,' he said, 'I thought we were going to be up half the night arguing about it.' He grinned down at her. 'That was *exactly* my own judgement, too,' he said. 'You see—two minds with but a single thought!'

Candida smiled back, glad that they'd agreed, glad that she'd done as he'd asked, and glad that the matter had all been sorted at last. Now, perhaps, he would go home and leave her in peace to have a bath and go to bed.

Just then her phone rang, and, answering it, she heard Faith's voice.

'Candida? You *have* kept next Sunday free, haven't you?' the woman said eagerly. 'Remember it's Maxy's big launch on Tuesday,' she went on, 'and he's coming here for a nice quiet family day—and a roast—and a long, long walk in the woods. If you're with us as well, it will be just perfect! I'm going to do a couple of duck-lings. We'll keep your cawl for another time!'

Candida couldn't help smiling at Faith's exuberance. Did anyone ever turn down Faith's requests? she wondered. Well, she'd have to go, she thought. She'd *have* to keep in with this family until Max's apartment was finished. She looked up at him.

'It's your sister,' she mouthed quietly. Then, 'Thank you, Faith…that would be lovely.'

'Wonderful—and Maxy will be bringing you, so there's no need for you to drive yourself here,' Faith added. 'We'll expect you both in time for morning coffee.'

So the plan was already in place, Candida thought. All cut and dried. And she was going along with it…as usual!

They rang off, and Max looked down at her. 'I take it that was all about Sunday? Good.' He glanced at his watch. 'Go and get ready. I'm taking you out to dinner,' he said. 'I think you need some well-earned nourishment.'

'Oh…I don't want to eat out tonight,' Candida began. 'It's too late for me, and anyway—' He interrupted.

'Well, we'll have to stay here, then. We can cook something.' He sat down. 'I feel like celebrating because I'm so thankful that I can give back those stories knowing I've made the right choice.'

Candida looked down at him. 'I can't cook anything worthwhile because I haven't been shopping yet this week….'

'Then it's a good job I booked a table for nine-thirty at the Firehouse Grill around the corner,' he said briefly.

Candida bit her lip. He was so sure of himself, she thought. So sure she'd do exactly as he wanted! 'And if I…refuse your kind offer?' she began

'Oh, I considered that—but thought you'd probably agree to come in the end,' he replied easily. 'Come on,' he murmured in his most cajoling tone, 'if you don't want to eat anything you can sit and watch *me*.'

He stood up and came over to her, longing to pull her towards him, to kiss her mouth and touch her eyelids with his lips. He knew very well that she'd been crying before he'd arrived earlier. Something had upset her, and it had upset *him* to see her looking so defenceless—and so desirable! He looked away for a second. Since Candida had arrived on the scene she'd altered his plans. He knew that he wanted to have Candida at his side, long-term. Was aware that they had that inexplicable 'something' that could draw two people together in a union which, hopefully, might last a lifetime. And—most amazingly of all—he was in *love* again, for the first time in years! How had *that* happened?

CHAPTER TEN

CANDIDA woke early, and lay staring up at the ceiling. Today was her father's birthday, and she was relieved that she'd recovered from her recent bout of flu in time to celebrate it with him.

Since that fantastic Sunday she'd spent with Max and the family at Farmhouse Cottage, Candida had not seen him at all, though he'd rung her several times. Thankfully, his new novel had been launched to huge acclaim, and sales had gone through the roof almost at once. After reading the glowing reviews, she'd rung to congratulate him, and the elation in his voice had been tangible—yet cautious.

'Of course I'm very…relieved…' he'd said. 'But there's always the next one to worry about!' He'd paused. 'I'm obliged to be all over the place book signing for the next couple of weeks….but what I'd really like, just at this moment, is a quiet meal at Edouard's—just you and me. But that'll have to wait, I'm afraid.'

After they'd finished speaking Candida had sat for a long time, her head in her hands. Every time she talked to him, every time she thought about him, it was making it worse. She just could not stop him crowding her thoughts. And her dilemma now was the same as it had always been: .how could she bring herself to tell him about the matter of her book—or, alternatively, how could she *not* tell him? When she was with him she could forgive and actually forget the wretched business, but when she was alone that persistent resentment *would* keep surfacing, like a recurring fever for which there was no cure. Where was her guardian angel? she asked herself.

Then, a week later, she'd gone down with a bad attack of flu, and for the next four weeks she hadn't really left the flat. Max had rung, and sent flowers, but any suggestion about making time to come and visit her had met with strong opposition from Candida. For one thing, she'd lost her voice completely for days, and for another she hadn't wanted anyone—especially *him*— seeing her so washed out, white-faced and red-nosed! Perhaps, she'd thought, as she'd dragged herself from bedroom, to bathroom, to kitchen, to prepare a hot drink now and then, this enforced separation was a blessing in disguise. If she didn't see him, if she didn't let those penetrating eyes work their magic, it would be easier one day soon—as soon as she'd completed the work for him—to cast herself adrift once and for all.

Now, Candida threw back her duvet and reached for her dressing gown. She really must concentrate on today, she scolded herself. Let thoughts of Maximus Seymour take a back seat for once! If that was possible! This was her father's sixtieth birthday, and she'd make sure it was a good one.

She showered and changed into jeans and a black sweater, before packing her small overnight case which contained the aquamarine silk dress she'd worn to

Faith's party—the dress that Max had been so compli-
mentary about. She tutted. *Damn* Max! she thought.
Why did she have to refer to *him*? She knew her dad
would like it…that was all that mattered!

Then she took the large birthday cake she'd made
from the cupboard, and looked at it again with a critical
eye. Her father loved a rich fruitcake, and Candida had
taken care with the icing of it, the decoration on the top
and sides demonstrating his love of rugby football and
music. She couldn't help feeling pleased as she placed
it carefully into the strong cardboard box she'd purchased. She'd really enjoyed making the cake, and it had
baked to a beautiful, perfect shape.

Candida reckoned on starting her journey at eight,
and as it was now only seven-fifteen there was plenty
of time for her to make her toast and coffee. She was
just spooning some grounds into the percolator when
her internal door buzzer sounded, and she glanced up,
smiling. That would be her friendly neighbour from
downstairs, to wish her a good time, she thought. The
girl had been very helpful and attentive to Candida when
she'd been so unwell.

Throwing open the door, Candida was astonished—
and almost gasped out loud—to see Max standing in
front of her, a strong brown paper carrier in his hands.

He gazed down, his lips slightly parted in a faint
smile. 'Front door was open,' he explained, 'so I was
able to come straight up the stairs.' He paused. 'I knew
I'd be in time to catch you before you went, and I also
hoped there'd be a cup of coffee going.'

'Oh, Max…of course… Please…come in!' Candida

didn't like to ask him what on earth he was doing here, but she didn't have to. He interrupted her thoughts.

'Before you ask,' he said cheerfully, 'I'm here bearing gifts.' He put the bag down on the kitchen surface. 'Just a little contribution towards the birthday celebrations.'

The 'little contribution' turned out to be two bottles of the best champagne, and Candida was almost overwhelmed at the gesture—not to mention unnerved at Max's unexpected arrival!

'Honestly, Max…you shouldn't—I mean, there was no need…' she began.

'Oh, I think there was,' he said. 'For one thing, you did me a huge favour with the short stories, and for another sixty is an important milestone in anyone's life.' He grimaced briefly. '*I'm* going to be forty—next Valentine's Day, as a matter of fact.' He glanced down at the box with the cake in it, which Candida still hadn't closed and taped down. 'You didn't make that, did you, Candida?' he asked.

'All my own work,' Candida said non-committally.

Max studied it for a second or two. 'That's brilliant,' he said, genuinely impressed. 'Really professional.' He grinned down at her. 'Can I place an order for my own event next year?'

Candida smiled and looked away, busying herself with the coffee. Next year was a long way off, she thought, and by the fourteenth of February she wanted Max Seymour's presence in her life to be history.

Max refused her offer of toast, but helped himself to a second cup of coffee before helping her gather together everything that she was taking with her.

'Let me carry it all down for you,' he said, picking up her case, her coat and large umbrella, and hooking the bag with the champagne in over his arm.

Candida glanced around the flat briefly, to make sure she'd not forgotten anything, then went out, locking her door and following him downstairs. Outside, Max had packed everything neatly into the boot of her car, wedging the precious cake safely so that it wouldn't move on the journey, and tucking the champagne inside the car rug.

'There,' he said, standing back. 'That should all be OK.' He glanced at his watch. 'What time is your father expecting you?'

'By lunchtime,' Candida replied. She looked up at Max, her heart missing a beat. Even on this rather dismal December morning he looked as seductive as ever, dressed in an open-neck shirt and a casual leather jacket. She made herself look away! 'Thanks again for my dad's present, Max…it's very generous of you.'

He opened the door for her, and Candida got in and switched on the ignition. But after one pathetic wheeze it died—totally! Candida was horrified!

'Oh, no!' she exclaimed. 'Not today—*please*!' She waited for a minute, then tried again. This time it was worse than ever. There was no life there at all!

She looked up through the open window at Max. 'I don't believe this,' she said helplessly. 'What d'you think can be wrong? I'm useless at anything mechanical,' she added.

Max shrugged. 'Could be anything,' he said, rather unhelpfully. 'Battery, perhaps?'

'Can't be that,' Candida said firmly. 'I only had a new one last month.'

After several more fruitless tries at getting the thing started, Candida leaned her head on the steering wheel for a second. The best laid plans of mice and men! she thought.

Max looked down at her, smiling inwardly. He could offer to tinker about with the thing, he thought—he had jump leads in his car, and could probably quite easily get Candida's car started—but it wouldn't be good if she broke down on her journey later, he thought. Then his fertile mind swung into action.

'Look, it's Saturday morning. You're not going to get anyone to come out very promptly,' he said. He paused, hoping he was choosing the right moment. 'There's only one thing for it,' he said, 'I'll have to take you in my car.'

Candida stared up at him. 'Max—don't be silly— you can't possibly do that! It's a long way, and—'

'My car is quite used to going long distances,' he pointed out dryly.

'Yes, but I'm staying overnight… Surely you've other things to do? It's going to mean the whole weekend wasted for you, and—'

'At least for a while my time's my own—to do what I like with,' he said. 'Come on—let's be decisive. This is an important day—you don't want to let everyone, let your father down. Out you come. We'll transfer everything into my car and be on our way.'

He turned and went around to the boot before Candida could say another word, and although all her instincts were running riot, warning her to refuse his very thoughtful offer, she felt tremendously relieved. At least in Max's vehicle they'd be sure to arrive! She must do something about changing hers soon, she thought. It *had* been on the blink lately. She should have heeded all those warning signs.

Deftly, Max packed everything into his car, and within a very few minutes they were driving off towards the motorway.

Leaning back in her seat, Candida said suddenly, 'What about Ella? Isn't she at home?'

'Funnily enough, the Jarretts asked if they could have her for the weekend,' he said. 'Their young grandson is staying with them, and he adores the dog. So they're all going on some long walks.' He glanced across at Candida briefly. 'The Jarretts are very good to me, so I fall in with their wishes when I can—and Ella's not complaining!'

Feeling slightly dazed at the turn of events, Candida allowed herself to sit and enjoy the ride. Even if this *was* totally unplanned, she had to admit that she never enjoyed the journey to Wales—and sailing along the Tarmac in Max's Mercedes was another matter entirely!

Suddenly she froze as her mind ran ahead. What about tonight? she asked herself. She couldn't possibly ask Max to stay at her father's modest abode. Yet it would be very unfriendly to suggest that he stayed at the local hostelry—a pub called the Three Bells, which did have a couple of rooms. She bit her lip. How on earth was all this going to pan out? she thought desperately.

Once again, as if able to read her mind, Max said casually, 'I take it there's somewhere local I can rest my head tonight?'

'Well, there is the local pub,' Candida replied. 'Nothing very grand, I'm afraid, Max—but the accommodation is OK, I believe.'

'That'll do me fine,' he said briefly, not looking at her. He didn't care where he slept for his usual four or five hours! He was just glad he hadn't made any plans for this weekend. Suddenly the whole idea of taking Candida to visit her father, and joining the birthday party, appealed to Max. It would be an experience, and it could turn out to be fun, he thought. But the best thing of all was that he would be with Candida. He had missed her company, had missed seeing her over the last month, and although part of that had been due to his commitments, she'd seemed to have made herself inaccessible to him. It was true she'd been quite ill but still, he definitely had the feeling she'd been keeping him at arm's length, and had been rather cool towards him.

At about midday, after having stopped for a rest and some refreshment at a motorway services station, they pulled up outside the small end-of-terrace family house where Candida had been brought up. For the last forty miles or so of the journey, since leaving the motorway, Candida had been gratified at Max's reaction to the scenery that had unfolded around them as they drove. A pale, wintry sun had at last started to filter through the trees, lighting up the stonework of the pretty ancient church and the war memorial as they made their way slowly through the narrow roads of the village.

Looking across at him, she could see that he was genuinely interested in everything as they drove—and she was strangely pleased. Then she shrugged. This would be a one-off occasion, and whether he liked it or not was irrelevant. But she would always be grateful to him for rescuing her from her plight earlier. It would have messed up everything if she'd had to come by train and then get someone to pick her up, with all her stuff, from the station twelve miles away. Coming home by any other means of transport than car was a lengthy nightmare. She'd only ever done it once before, and had vowed never to repeat the experience!

They'd only just started getting out of the car when the front door of the house opened and Freddy, Candida's father, emerged—running down the path towards them, with Toby the Jack Russell scampering at his heels. He was a short, stocky, dark-skinned man, with black wavy hair, and his joy at seeing his daughter was obvious from the tears that formed quickly in his twinkly blue eyes as he hugged her.

'Dad!' she said, as he nearly squeezed the breath from her body. 'Dad—happy birthday, Dad!'

Freddy held her away from him for a second. 'It will be, now you're here,' he said.

Candida bent to make a fuss of the dog, then turned quickly to introduce the two men. 'This is Max, Dad…we met a few weeks ago, on business,' she said quickly. 'And you'll never guess—my car refused to start this morning, and by a huge stroke of luck Max turned up and insisted on bringing me!' She looked up at Max, who was observing the two of them with a strange look on his face. 'Max—this is Freddy—my lovely dad,' she said simply.

Freddy took Max's hand, grasping it tightly. 'Well, well, well,' he said. 'So you're the knight in shining armour, then, are you?' He looked over at the Mercedes. 'And what a great charger you've got there, Max! My word—that's what you *call* a car!'

Max crouched down to talk to the dog, glancing up

at Candida. 'This is a cute creature,' he said. 'D'you think Toby and Ella would like each other?'

Presently, they all went into the house, Max's tall frame almost filling the small hallway as he followed Candida. Candida felt her pulse going crazy. What on earth would he think of this little abode? she asked herself. She knew that of course her father always kept everything very clean and tidy, but nothing had been updated for years, and the whole effect could only be classed as homely. But still, Candida thought as she glanced around her, this was the place she'd loved, and still loved, and Max could think what he liked…his opinion wasn't important!

She glanced up to see him looking at her with a quizzical expression on his face, and she smiled automatically. 'Well, this is where I was brought up, Max,' she began. 'Not *exactly* what you were used to—'

He cut in. 'It seems a lovely family home to me,' he said slowly. He glanced over her head towards the window. 'And what a view…a field—with sheep!'

After a few minutes' conversation about the journey, Freddy said, 'Now, then, let's fetch all your things in from the car.'

Max said quickly, 'There's only your daughter's to worry about, because I am as you see me, Freddy. I had no idea I would be coming along today, so of course I didn't pack anything.'

'No worries,' Freddy said. 'I can let you have anything you might need later, Max.'

Candida interrupted hastily. 'I thought there'd be room at the Three Bells for Max tonight, Dad. I'll give them a ring in a minute,' she said, but was silenced by the look on her father's face.

'What are you talking about, girl?' he demanded. 'We do not send visitors to stay at pubs—not when there's a perfectly good room vacant here in the house!' He turned to Max. 'I always keep the spare bed made up, just in case,' he added. 'And you are very welcome, Max.'

Candida flushed in acute embarrassment! She hadn't anticipated for a second that Max would be staying *here*…though there was nothing wrong with the place, she admitted. It just seemed bizarre for sophisticated Maximus Seymour to be spending the night in their minute box room, with its chintzy furnishings. And she could hardly offer him her own, larger room, because it was even less appropriate, with frills everywhere and her resident array of teddy bears and cuddly toys sitting all over the place!

'Perhaps, Dad, Max would be happier staying at the pub—' she began, but Max cut in straight away.

'No, I wouldn't, thanks,' he said flatly. He turned to Freddy. 'I've had hotels up to here,' he said. 'My work often takes me away from home, and for the last few weeks I've hardly slept in my own bed at all. So I'm very glad to accept your offer, Freddy.'

So that was that. As he and Candida went back down the path to fetch everything, she said, 'I'm sure you'd really rather stay at the pub, Max. My dad can be very persuasive at times.'

'And I'm sure I really would not,' Max said. He caught her arm for a second. 'Relax, Candida. I realise I'm an unexpected addition to your day, but I'm here now, and there's nothing you can do about it. I have the feeling I'm going to enjoy myself this evening.' He paused. 'And your father is…a lovely man,' he added.

That did it! In a flash Max had gone up in Candida's estimation, because she'd always worshipped her father and it was good when someone else—a complete stranger—obviously liked him as well.

As they leaned into the boot, Max said, 'Didn't you say the party is to be a surprise? How is that going to happen?'

'Yes, it is a surprise, and it's all set up in the village hall,' Candida explained. 'But Dad thinks we're just going to his best friend's house for a few drinks. Just before we leave to go up there, we'll get a phone call asking us to collect something from the hall—and when we arrive about a hundred people will start singing "Happy Birthday"!'

Max was impressed. 'Your father must be a very popular man,' he said.

'Oh, everyone knows Dad,' Candida said. 'They've all helped out. The local butcher has cooked the hams, and is providing his own famously special sausages… And don't look like that, Max…'

'What d'you mean? I'm not looking like anything,' Max said, hurt.

'Yes, you are. I don't expect sausages would appear on the menu for one of *your* parties, but my dad loves them, and it's his party……'

Max put his arm around Candida's waist and pulled her roughly towards him. 'Don't put words into my mouth, Candida,' he said, in a surprisingly terse tone. 'And don't try and dissect my feelings, either. There's nothing wrong with good home-cooked food.' He paused. 'I don't know why you have such a—strange opinion of me,' he added.

Candida caught her breath, realising that she'd better

do as he said and try and relax. Because if she didn't she'd be responsible for causing unnecessary tension—between him and herself—and she wanted the occasion to be special for her father.

She turned away without responding to his last remark. 'We've ordered barrels of beer, and everything else is being sorted by the wives of my dad's friends…you know, salads and stuff. And there's going to be gorgeous puddings!' She watched as Max picked up the cake. 'Dad knows that I've baked his cake,' she said, 'so we can take that in with us now—together with your champagne, Max. He'll be amazed!'

After they'd gone back into the house, and Freddy had admired the cake and Max's extravagant gift, the older man said, 'Well, lunch is ready…you must both be starving!'

Candida looked up at Max, a half-smile on her face. She knew what they were going to be eating, because she'd smelt it as soon as they'd arrived! And as they took their seats at the dining room table, and Freddy carried in the huge pan of scalding food, Max glanced at Candida, one dark eyebrow raised.

'Is it…? Can it be…?' he murmured.

'This is our speciality,' Freddy announced proudly, as he began to ladle generous helpings into deep soup bowls. 'This is cawl—and I hope you like it, Max.' He added, 'Or perhaps you've never even heard of it!'

'Oh…I've heard of it, Freddy,' Max said easily, picking up his spoon. 'And don't worry about me—I know I'm going to enjoy every single mouthful!'

CHAPTER ELEVEN

'I'M REALLY sorry, Max—I forgot to warn you that we might expect this!' Candida looked across at Max as they began their return journey the following afternoon. Heavy rain was pouring relentlessly from grey and leaden skies, and the windscreen wipers were working overtime to allow Max to see the road ahead. He glanced back at her.

'Oh, I never allow the weather to bother me too much,' he said flatly. 'Ella and I seem to be permanently soaking from about November to March on our walks—in fact, she revels in getting wet and then shaking herself all over me.'

'Yes, but Welsh rain is so much wetter than you get anywhere else,' Candida said. 'And there's always a lot more of it! Dad said this started at three in the morning.' She paused. 'And poor Toby hasn't had his walk yet today either—Dad'll have to see to it later. I had hoped we all might have gone out, but there didn't seem any point in us getting soaked and then having to sit in the car in damp clothes.'

'It'd have been OK if I'd had something to change into,' Max said, 'but I didn't.'

Candida looked across at him quickly, his words reminding her that if it hadn't been for him turning up unexpectedly and insisting on bringing her here yesterday she would probably not have managed it at all. 'I can't thank you enough for getting me here,' she said. 'I've been thinking about it, and I suppose the only thing open to me would have been to hire another car. But—'

'But as it happened there was no need to do that,' he cut in. 'Since one arrived at your door, complete with chauffeur.'

Candida sat back and gazed out of the window. Her father's party had been a fantastic success, not finishing until after one a.m. And then later, at home, Freddy had insisted on opening one of the bottles of champagne. No wonder she felt somewhat fragile today, Candida thought—and even Max didn't seem himself either. His attitude was rather…how could she describe it? Distant? Perhaps he was always like this after a party? she thought.

'I don't think my father could get over last night,' she said now, looking across at Max. 'It really had been kept a total secret from him, which is rather amazing, don't you think?'

'Yes. In fact, the whole event was…rather amazing,' Max said slowly, as he waited at a crossroads before pulling away again. He remembered how wonderful, how exquisite Candida had looked in that dress he'd first seen her in, and how proud of her Freddy so obviously was. 'I've never been to anything like that before…so traditional,' he said. 'A village hall bedecked with bunting and balloons…'

Candida looked away briefly. Was he being patronising? she asked herself.

'Well, everything went exactly as planned,' she said. 'And the food was super, wasn't it? I do hope you had enough to eat,' she added.

'Oh, Freddy made sure I was well supplied,' he said. 'And, yes, it was all delicious. And I thought the serving wenches were all…lovely ladies.'

Candida had to smile. The women who'd taken charge of the supper arrangements were all more or less her father's age, or older, but that hadn't stopped them admiring the very handsome stranger in their midst. As soon as Max had entered the room he'd generated a buzz of interest, and although it didn't matter a jot to *her*, Candida had had to admit to a certain feeling of possessive pride. He was with *her*…just for now…and naturally was the most dishy man present As he'd stood with his pint mug in his hand, his dark eyes roaming the room, that heart-throbbing half-smile playing on his sensuous lips, Candida had almost been able to hear the collective sigh from every female breast!

'Your father is a great bloke,' Max said suddenly. 'I can readily understand why you're so close…you've obviously got a great relationship.'

'Dad and I often seem to share the same opinions,' Candida said. 'But I've always been allowed to do my own thing…he's never put any pressure on me.' She paused. 'I'm afraid he does miss me—rather a lot—but he gets very loyal back-up from his friends, and the choir is a big part of his life.'

'They made a remarkable sound,' Max said at once. 'I'm not much into male voice choirs myself, and certainly never heard one up that close, that immediate. It was very touching at times. I thought.'

Candida raised her eyebrows slightly at that. She wouldn't have thought Max Seymour could be touched by anything—not in that way—and certainly not by thirty mature and rather portly men raising their voices in enthusiastic song. But what had touched *her* was seeing how much her father had so patently liked Max's company. While she'd been busy helping with everything at the other end of the hall, she'd glanced across from time to time to see the two men chatting amiably, and had noticed Max throw his head back, laughing at something her father had said. Freddy was known as a joker, with a quick wit.

'And the barn dance—that went down well too, didn't it?' Candida said, wanting to extend the evening by talking about it. 'Although not *everyone* joined in,' she added pointedly.

'I admit that I decided to decline that opportunity,' Max said levelly. 'And anyway, you didn't take part either, did you?'

'I was cutting up the birthday cake at that point,' Candida protested. 'I was so pleased that there was enough for everyone to have a small bit, and some left over for Dad to take home and keep in his cake tin.'

They drove in silence for a while, Candida's mind going over and over all the details of the occasion. Of *course* she would not have expected Max to join in the barn dance…that would have been one unsophisticated step too far! But she wasn't complaining—about *anything*. Even the lunch they'd had today at the Three Bells—which Freddy had insisted should be his treat— had been surprisingly good. At least nothing awful had happened to embarrass her, she thought, and if Max had felt the whole thing was beneath him, he hadn't shown it. Anyway, it had not been *her* idea that he was there at all, and he'd assured her—and assured her father—that he'd had a great time. But then, he would, wouldn't he? she thought. You could never be sure with Max—his way with words could convince anybody of anything. She sighed briefly. Well, it was all over. Done and dusted. Now she had her immediate future to think about.

Max cut in on her thoughts. 'Are you going home for Christmas?' he asked casually, knowing very well that of course she would be.

'Oh, Dad and I have never had a Christmas apart yet,' Candida replied promptly, and, to be polite, said, 'What about you? Do you spend the festive season with Faith and Rick?'

He paused before answering. 'I'm always invited,' he replied, 'but sometimes Ella and I don't go until Boxing Day, or the day after…'

'So—since you are apparently not capable of boiling yourself an egg,' Candida said, 'What d'you do about Christmas Day lunch?'

'There's always Edouard's,' he said flatly.

Candida bit her lip for a second, looking away, suddenly feeling sorry for rich and gorgeous Maximus Seymour. He was a lonely man, she thought, in spite of Faith's loyalty. But surely if he was lonely it must be his own fault. There must have been a long line of women in his life who'd have been happy to call themselves Mrs Seymour.

Throwing discretion to the winds, she said, 'Why did you never marry, Max?'

'Oh, I did,' he replied, without looking at her.

Well, *that* was a revelation! No one had ever hinted that Max had had a wife!

'Kelly and I were married for precisely one year. But, as I think I may have said before, writers make rotten partners. Kelly certainly thought so. I suppose we were happy enough for a couple of months, but after that it was downhill all the way.' The dark eyebrows knitted briefly. 'What Kelly most enjoyed was mixing with the rich and famous—and having plenty of money to spend. That was what turned her on. She could never understand why I needed long hours of solitude—couldn't accept that for a time a book can take over a writer's life, leaving very little to give to others. To sit at home and be satisfied with the unspectacular was not what Kelly wanted to do.'

Candida looked away. She would never have expected Max to talk to her like this...to say very personal things about his life, his past. And she felt that he had allowed her to intrude into a very private area.

'And the best—or the worst—of it was,' he went on, 'that when we first met and were getting to know each other she claimed to have read all my books and "adored" all of them. Her words. But that was a total lie. It was easy enough to find that out, and prove that she'd never got past page one of any of them! Didn't have a clue. When I challenged her, she admitted it.' He braked sharply, to avoid a rabbit running across the road in front of them, before going on, 'Of course I didn't care a toss about whether she'd read my stuff or not.' He paused. 'But I cared that she'd lied about it.'

Candida's mind leapt back to the time he'd asked her the same questions.

'But that episode in my life is over—gone—and it's something we never talk about, anyway,' he said, as if to warn her that now that he'd confided in her that should be the end of it. He glanced across at her for a second. 'Enough about me...what kind of man will eventually capture your heart, Candida? Who's going to be able to tie *you* down emotionally?'

She looked at him squarely. 'Oh, the sort of man that most women are looking for, I suppose,' she replied.

'And that is?'

She paused. 'He must be utterly dependable, trust-worthy...and leave his roving eye on the altar steps. And...' She hesitated. 'He must always choose his words carefully, so as not to inflict unnecessary pain. He must realise that what he says, the words he uses, can be as damaging as sword-thrusts.'

Max frowned. 'That last demand is a bit of a tough call,' he said. 'Are you suggesting that he should take every word out of his mouth before uttering it for perhaps twenty, thirty—forty years?' Max's lip curled at the thought. 'I don't know any human being who could promise that,' he added.

'Well, a human being could try,' Candida replied bluntly. 'What I'm suggesting merely amounts to con-sideration for someone's feelings. And practise makes perfect.'

Candida closed her eyes for a few moments, suddenly feeling sleepy, but immediately opened them again at Max's next comment—or command!

'Seeing that I came to your party,' he said, 'you must agree to come to mine.'

She turned to face him. 'What party is that?'

'The one my publisher always throws at Christmas,' he said. He glanced at her, thinking how well her high-necked white sweater suited her. And her hair, obviously freshly shampooed, falling in soft waves around her shoulders, made him want to run his fingers through it, made him want to take hold of it and use it to pull her towards him. Instead, he looked back at the road ahead. 'It's held on the eighteenth of December.' He paused. 'This year it also happens to coincide with the fiftieth anniversary of my publishing company. I hope you're not already booked up,' he said, in a rather headmasterly tone of voice.

Candida looked away for a second. She'd made up her mind that this weekend should be *the* absolute end—the grand finale as far as spending free time with him was concerned. Their business arrangements were a simple matter, and could be finished in a matter of days as soon as everything she'd ordered was in stock. Yet now it seemed there was *another* social occasion to contend with!

'I'm not sure when I'm going home yet,' she said, knowing full well that she never left London before at least the twentieth of December. 'Dad likes me there in good time to put up all the decorations and—don't laugh—we still do Christmas. There's always a real tree in the sitting room.'

'I'm not laughing,' he said. 'I'm sure Christmas in your house is a wonderful occasion. Balloons and everything, no doubt.'

Candida thought, Yes, Max! We *do* have balloons—lots of them! Her dad loved blowing them all up and hanging them from every ceiling!

'But surely you don't need to leave before the eighteenth?' he persisted.

Candida sighed. This was proving more difficult than she'd imagined. Max had been so good to her this weekend, and had been the perfect guest in every way—even if something in his manner now made her think that he couldn't wait to get back to London—and real life! 'What sort of a party is it?' she asked, trying not to sound off-hand.

'It's always a very generous affair,' he replied. 'And this year it's going to be held at the Savoy. Black tie, naturally, and the meal is always a multi-course extravaganza. I think you might quite enjoy it. For a few of us rooms are booked for the night, by the way,' he added. 'Because the evening does go on a bit.' He glanced across at her. 'There are always lots of interesting people in the book world there, of course, and they're sure to be well represented this year in view of the anniversary.' He paused. 'It would be a change for me to have someone…different…at my side,' he added, as an afterthought.

So—*his* party was going to be at one of the most famous and luxurious hotels in London, with everything laid on and experienced staff hovering to meet every need! Candida suddenly felt rattled. Her mind was still full of *their* do last night, full of the memory of comfortable friends who'd been perfectly happy to queue at the long trestle tables for home-made food! The contrast between that and what Max had just described couldn't have been greater, and Candida shuddered as she thought again of the modest village hall—which could actually do with a bit of a make-over, she admitted—with locally brewed beer literally on tap, rather than the high-quality wines that Max always drank. She almost shrank back in her seat for a second. *Whatever* he'd said about enjoying himself, she thought, he'd probably felt thoroughly uncomfortable last night—even though he'd made an excellent job of hiding the fact! It would not have been the sort of thing he *could* appreciate, and the more she thought of him resting his superior head on the single bed in their minute spare room, rather than in an opulent hotel, the more she felt almost sick! She didn't even want to imagine what would have gone through his head!

'By the way,' she said suddenly, 'what did you think of Dad's cawl? I know you *said* you enjoyed it—but what did you *really* think of it?' And why did she care?

Max hesitated for a second. 'It was a very…nourishing…satisfying…meal after our journey,' he began. She interrupted.

'You haven't answered my question.'

He sighed, not wanting to give the wrong impression. 'I'm actually not a great lover of stews,' he admitted reluctantly, 'so…'

'So—go on.'

'Well, if there was a choice, I don't suppose I'd select a stew…that's all.'

So! He *didn't* like it! Well, tough! To her, it was the meal that spoke of home and warmth and comfort! But she *had* asked for his honest opinion, and she knew very well that Max Seymour always expressed himself directly and to the point. So what else did she expect?

There was a long silence after that. Then, 'I'll have to check the date in my diary and let you know about your…party…' she said briefly. 'But—thanks for the invite.'

She closed her eyes again, not wanting to look at him. He was such a contradictory combination of arrogance and sometimes fleeting vulnerability that her own position was in a permanent state of flux. They'd been born into such different worlds. Hers could never match up to his. How could a relationship like that last? she asked herself realistically. He'd tire of her, and her background. Oh, yes, he'd *seemed* to enjoy himself yesterday, with her father and his friends and the unusual atmosphere of the birthday occasion, but it was purely the novelty that had been the attraction. Candida was absolutely certain of that.

He glanced across at her, seeing that her eyes were closed, but knowing that she wasn't asleep. She seemed upset today, he thought—and his somewhat negative comments about Freddy's stew, so thoughtfully provided, probably hadn't helped! Then he shrugged. As in most things, food was surely a subjective topic. And she *did* ask…

It was still raining as if it would never stop, and daylight was almost non-existent. They were just about a mile from the motorway when a low-slung sports car came rapidly up behind to within a mere foot of them, then swung out to overtake on an almost blind bend, causing water from the flooded road to shoot up from its wheels in a spectacular arc, flinging spray against the windscreen of the Mercedes as it roared past. Cursing volubly, Max automatically pulled up to give it space, careering to the left and braking sharply, almost hitting the hedge just as another vehicle came from the opposite direction towards them, flashing its lights and blasting the horn. It was the closest Candida had ever been to witnessing or being involved in a terrible accident, and her mouth went dry. The expression on Max's face was indescribable!

'What the *hell* was that youngster *thinking* about?' he exploded. 'Did he have a death wish for himself— and all of us? Or is that the normal way people drive down here?'

Candida's heart was still racing with fear as she dwelt for a second on what might have been—then she turned to Max, relief that they hadn't been hurt making her blurt out her words defensively. 'I don't know what you mean by "people down here",' she said shakily. 'That idiot could have been *anyone*! Haven't you ever seen bad driving in London? And don't bother to answer that!'

What a stupid remark for Max to have made, Candida thought hotly. Yet she was aware that the incident had shaken him, really shaken him, and for the first time ever she'd seen him look fearful and afraid. But—more than that—he was *angry*! Candida trembled slightly again. She'd never seen him look like that before!

They reached the motorway without further problems, and joined the long stream of traffic making its way towards the capital. Candida realised that neither of them had uttered a word for several miles, and, feeling more calm now, looked across at him, feeling regretful that a complete stranger seemed to have put a further damper on things—because Max was still very quiet, and still very cross!

'Are you…do you have a busy week ahead?' she asked lightly.

Before she could say anything more, he replied, 'Yes. And I need to get back now, as soon as possible.' He paused. 'I've got some catching up to do.'

So, that said it all, Candida thought. No mention of supper somewhere. Clearly he had no wish to extend this weekend—even with a final cup of coffee together! Suit yourself, she thought, staring ahead.

They arrived at her flat just after seven, and, although Max had indicated that he didn't want to hang around, he insisted on carrying her belongings upstairs for her. Putting her things down, he went across to the window, staring out into the street below. If this woman had been hurt earlier—while she was in *his* care—he'd never have forgiven himself, he thought, his mind still festering over the incident on the road. It had nearly been a tragic accident in which they could both have been killed.

Candida came over uncertainly to stand by his side, her large eyes troubled as she studied his features. It *had* been different today, she told herself. No—*he* had been different. Yesterday's relaxed, intimate atmosphere had all been an illusion, because now Max's face had that hard, granite look which she'd observed once or twice before...full of a brooding inwardness which no one would ever be able to interpret. But Candida was beginning to know the man—had been with him enough times to sense that something was going on inside that masterful head. And tonight, although the rain had at last stopped, the damp, melancholy atmosphere seemed to touch everything around them.

She felt, instinctively, that the last forty-eight hours would prove to be the end of their fleeting association...which, of course, was what she *wanted*! What was *sensible*! Yet in her private imaginings hadn't she seen herself beside him? Walking with him, talking with him, listening to him—and at times hotly *disagreeing* with him. Oh, yes, he'd never rob her of her independent spirit! But most of all she'd imagined being with him at night, being cradled in his arms, seeing that rugged profile beside her on the pillow, tracing its outline with her finger and gently easing away the frown lines on the broad forehead. And feeling his sensuous lips on hers, overtaking her completely.

But today was today. Her guardian angel had been at work! Max had been given the opportunity to know everything about her and her little life, and would now have been warned that it was a waste of time attempting to draw her into his own often dizzying world He would know it all…except for that one big thing that had bugged her for so long and which would never, never go away.

While these fleeting thoughts had kept her mind occupied for a few seconds, Max had been gazing down at her with a strange look in his eyes—and now, returning his look, Candida was more than ever convinced. Why would he need a woman like her when he had numerous others to call upon who were far more to his natural taste? Women who didn't mind being picked up and dropped as it suited him. And, anyway, there were always his fictional women to keep his mind occupied. He'd said that they were his soul mates, and Candida believed him.

He bent his head slightly, as if he was about to say something, and Candida lifted her face. He would probably kiss her on both cheeks, she thought. The sort of thing that friends did, which never meant anything.

But he didn't kiss her on both cheeks. He didn't kiss her at all. He merely cupped her chin in his hands briefly, without smiling, then said casually, 'Well, I'm…glad…I was able to be of service this weekend.'

'And so am I! More than I can say! Thank you again, Max,' Candida said lightly.

He paused. 'No need for thanks…it was my pleasure. It was…' he hesitated. 'An unusually enlightening experience,' he added.

Releasing her quickly, he moved away and went towards the door. 'Um…I'll be in touch in due course,' he said vaguely, and with that he was gone.

Candida heard the street door close, heard the Mercedes drive away into the night.

For a while she stood there, not knowing what to do, or what to think. Well, *that* was an abrupt ending to everything! she thought. So he'd been 'enlightened', had he? What was *that* supposed to mean—other than that he'd witnessed their little folksy gathering and found it an amusing experience? She lifted her chin. 'Don't call *me*, Max,' she said, out loud. 'I'll call *you*—when I can find the time!'

CHAPTER TWELVE

BACK home at his apartment, Max stared at the computer, his mind a seething mass of highly charged emotions. He had never been in such a personal tangle before in his life—not even when he and Kelly had split up. And now the saved data on the machine in front of him spelt out his predicament in no uncertain terms. He had a mountain to climb, he thought, and he hadn't even reached the foothills yet.

He stood up and went slowly across to the window, gazing out at the thousand lights of London twinkling in the darkness. That scene, so splendidly real, yet so strangely remote, usually gave him pleasure, comfort and inspiration, but tonight all he felt was sadness and a deep sense of regret—and the feeling that something, *someone* he wanted more than he'd ever wanted anything before in his life, was slowly drifting away from him to be permanently out of his reach.

He went out of his study and across to the drinks cabinet, where he poured himself a large whisky, his mind going over the events of the last two days. Yes, it had been a very unusual experience, he thought, and one which he'd actually loved every minute of. The warmth and goodwill he'd encountered, from first meeting Candida's father to mixing with the robust gathering at the party later, seeing how everyone was enjoying themselves, without a hint of pretentiousness or self-consciousness, had been refreshing. It must be like that in all small rural communities, he thought, where everyone knew everyone else.

But what he had loved most was being with Candida... Seeing her there, chatting animatedly with all her old friends and acquaintances, had made him feel curiously envious. Of course he, himself, had plenty of acquaintances, he thought, but most of them were not like that, so unaffected and down to earth, with no hidden agendas, no gushing with sycophantic hypocrisy. There was always Rob Winters, and a couple of other mates he saw from time to time, but he freely admitted that—like most men—he was not particularly good at relationships, not good at making the effort involved in keeping up with friends. Thank goodness he had Faith and Rick and Emily as his safety valve, he thought, twirling his glass between his finger and thumb for a second. It would be wonderful to own a retreat in the countryside like they had, he thought. Perhaps in the Welsh hills. To walk the dogs, Ella and Toby, for miles and miles across those rolling fields, maybe stop for a pint at the Three Bells, then go home with—

Max pulled himself up sharply from these flights of fancy. Stop it—stop it now, he told himself! All that could never be—not now, not ever. Unless some saint from heaven came and interceded for him!

Candida took a long look at herself in the mirror, feeling both glad and sorry to be here in this elegant bedroom at the hotel. When she and Max had stepped from the lift earlier, and walked along the hushed, heavily carpeted corridor, she'd been relieved to find that she'd been allotted a bedroom to herself—next to Max's She'd already worked out her plan of action if he assumed they'd be sharing! A plan which didn't include *him*!

She had finally—and reluctantly—agreed to accept Max's invitation to his big party. Well, they were already in the swing of the festive season, she'd reasoned, and she was never likely to have an opportunity like this again, and she really didn't want to let Faith down—the woman had been so excited about Candida attending the party. So she might as well take what was going—why look a gift horse in the mouth? she'd asked herself.

In the following couple of weeks after her father's party Candida had buried herself in her work, to keep her mind off things. Max had obviously been very busy, too, because she hadn't seen him at all—though he had rung twice. But when he had, he'd seemed off-hand...not like his usual self. Good, she'd thought. He was cooling off—as she'd known he would—and playing into her hands very well. Theirs was a doomed relationship. By the New Year she would be free of him altogether—free as a bird to make a fresh start.

And this party was to be the curtain-call on her association with Maximus Seymour. He had said 'black tie', which meant 'posh frock', but she'd decided against buying anything new. There was no point in going over the top. Besides, she knew very well that her long black evening gown—worn on two occasions when she'd been with Grant—suited her perfectly. Sleeveless, low-necked and figure hugging, with a slight flare towards the hemline to reveal her pretty ankles and high-heeled strappy shoes, it had the effect of somehow making her feel in control. And that was where she needed to be—at all times!

Candida checked her hair again. Tonight she'd piled it up on top of her head, using a gold clip to hold it in place, and her only jewellery was a pair of long gold earrings.

Just then there was a discreet tap at the door. Max stood there, the expression on his face when he took in her appearance making her want to look away in embarrassment.

'Come in—I'm almost ready,' she said airily, remembering that she hadn't yet put on her perfume.

He did as he was told, shutting the door behind him, and Candida, looking at him properly, had to catch her breath. She had never seen him in full evening dress before, and he was quite literally stunning, she admitted. His suit was expensive, elegantly cut, setting off his broad shoulders and strong physique to perfection. And the immaculate crisp white shirt gleamed against his tanned skin. He looked down at her, those black eyes glinting in the soft lighting, and his voice—that rich mix of throaty masculinity and seductiveness—made Candida annoyingly weak at the knees when he spoke.

'You look…fantastic…Candida,' he said slowly, and she looked up at him quickly.

'Thanks,' she said, then, 'And you look all right, too.'

She moved across the room away from him, to fetch her perfume, then sat on the edge of the bed for a moment, gently applying the scent to her neck and wrists. He came over to stand next to her.

'Before we go down,' he said slowly, 'I've a favour to ask, Candida.'

Candida looked up at him, her eyebrows raised in query. 'What's that?' she asked, her pulse quickening. It depended what it was!

'I'm stuck on one of my plots at the moment,' he said slowly, and Candida thought, So *that's* what's kept him busy lately.

'It's unusual for me not to know where a yarn is going,' he said, 'but this one has really got me stumped.' He frowned briefly. 'I thought you'd be just the person to get me out of a hole.'

Candida was relieved—although very surprised at his request. At least it didn't concern *her*, she thought gratefully, but the fact that Max Seymour—self-assured, successful novelist of renown—couldn't sort himself out and was once more asking for *her* help was incredible!

'Well, try me,' she said lightly. 'Though I'm not promising anything.'

He moved away and went across to the window, his hands in his pockets.

'I'll try and be brief,' he said, not looking at her. 'It's a "Beauty and the Beast" affair, really.' He waited before going on. 'There's this beautiful girl—a beautiful, innocent girl—and the unfortunate beast wants her more than anything else in the world. Life might have turned out OK for him in time, because the girl is kind and compassionate, and the beast thinks that she likes him well enough…well enough to overlook his many, many, drawbacks. But the problem is—and it is a massive problem—the beast unwittingly hurt her—really hurt her—a long time ago, even though it wasn't all his fault.

And he doesn't think that this girl—this truly beautiful girl—can ever forgive him. Forgive him enough to…love him. Because if she can't, the sad creature will probably die. So—where can he go from here?'

It was fortunate that Candida was sitting down on the bed, or her knees might have given way beneath her! Her quick mind had picked up his message. So he *knew*. Max knew her secret at last! But how? she asked herself.

She swallowed over a dry throat. 'Let's stop playing games for a minute, Max,' she said, as calmly as she could. 'I think I know the story you're telling me.'

He came over then, and knelt in front of her so that he could look straight into her eyes.

'Yes, you've known it for a lot longer than I have,' he said. 'You've had the advantage over me, which in this case is thoroughly deserved,' he added. 'But it's taken a visit to Wales and a sixtieth birthday party to enlighten me… Plus a revealing talk with Freddy to open my eyes.'

Candida bit her lip—how had *that* happened? she asked herself. The subject was no longer referred to at home, and her father had never mentioned it since that humiliating time.

'Freddy asked me what I did in life,' Max went on. 'I think he thought I was in the interior design business, like you. When I said that I wrote, he told me that *you* had always loved writing, too—had been scribbling away since childhood and had won prizes at school. He said that you had actually had a book published some years ago, but that there'd been such a scathing critique from "some swine of a reviewer" in one of the broad-

sheets that you'd given up in an agony of disillusionment. He told me what your *nom de plume* was…'

'I called myself Jane Llewellyn,' Candida said
quietly. 'My mother's name.' She paused, and looked
into Max's eyes for a long moment. 'How could you
have been so cruel to a new writer? Or to anyone?' she
asked quietly. But Candida realised that suddenly she
was not angry any more. It was too late for anger, she
thought. It was wasteful of her feelings. What was done,
was done. At least Max Seymour knew, now. And *she*
hadn't had to tell him, after all.

'I'm sorry. Yes, some of what I wrote was…hard…'
he agreed. 'I was able to retrieve my review notice on my
computer—with the information I had it was easy to
find—but what you don't realise is that they cut my last
paragraph from the newspaper.' He looked away for a
second, his expression dark. 'It's what editors do,' he said
brusquely. 'But what they left out was my final remarks,
which were, "But this writer shows huge overall promise,
and could be a highly successful novelist one day if she
allows herself time to grow up and develop the craft."'
He paused. 'God—what a patronising git I must have
sounded…must have *been*!' he groaned.

Max took her hands, holding them tightly in his, and
their faces were so close it would only have taken a split
second for their lips to meet. 'If you had been able to
read that last paragraph,' he said softly, 'it would have
made all the difference to you, wouldn't it, Candida? By
now you could have had half a dozen books published.
In fact, I could almost guarantee that you would have.'

Candida's eyes glistened in the mellow light from the
bedside lamps, her heart lifting at his words—the words

of encouragement that, indeed, might have changed the course of her life if she'd had the opportunity to read them!

'One of the things that struck me as so unfair at the time,' Candida said slowly, 'was that I knew very well that *you* had had every advantage. With a famous member of the family to give you advice, to help you over the difficult bits, to introduce you to all the right people…'

'*No!*' Max said, almost angrily, and Candida drew back in surprise. 'It wasn't *like* that!' He set his lips in the familiar terse way before going on. 'My mother had no interest in me whatsoever—not even as a person. Faith was her favourite. The only advice my mother ever gave me was to stick at it—not to be distracted. My books were treated with indifference. Of course, through her, I did meet other people in the trade, but I was never made a fuss of. It was my mother who was always in the limelight. Which is where she liked to be.' He paused. 'We just seemed to float about in the creative universe, hardly ever touching at all. It was a very odd thing—but I was anonymous to my mother. I barely existed. Or so it seemed to me.'

Candida was frankly amazed at his words. When she thought of all the love and support she'd always received at home, first from both her parents and, for much longer, from her father, in whatever she'd done in her life, it was difficult not to believe that everyone was treated in the same way.

'The thing is,' Max went on, 'can you ever forgive me, allow me to prove to you that although, yes, I'm capable of cruelty sometimes—thankfully usually expressed in fiction—I'd like to do anything, everything, to help you succeed, Candida?' When she didn't reply, he went on, 'Just think—we'd get another table for the study, the room's big enough for both of us, and we could write together, but apart. You'd have your own space to concentrate.' He paused for a second, gazing into her eyes, desperate to read her thoughts. 'That is what you'd like to do, isn't it, Candida?' he asked, a note of anxiety in his voice. 'It *is* still there, isn't it? The ambition to write?' He couldn't bear to think that *he* might have put a permanent stop to it.

'It has never gone away,' Candida said soberly.

'And it never will,' Max assured her. 'If it's in the blood, it's in the blood.'

There was silence for a moment, then Candida's common sense rushed at her in a flash. What was he doing, exactly? Offering her a corner of his apartment to write? How was she supposed to live? She had precious few savings!

'I can't afford to even consider it for the moment,' she said, releasing her hands from his. 'I've no money, and—'

He stared at her, frowning slightly, then smiled with that lazy movement of his desirable lips that always made Candida's nerves tingle. 'Don't you get it?' he asked softly. 'You little fool, Candida. You won't *need* money—I've got plenty for us both…' And, when she still didn't seem to understand, he said, 'I'm asking you to *marry* me, Candy. I want you to be my wife—my life.' Before she could interrupt, he went on, 'I love you, and I want us to be together always.'

She looked up at him quickly. He'd called her Candy for the very first time—the name used by everyone who knew her well and loved her!

Candida felt her head spinning. Was this a dream? Would she wake up in a minute and find herself in rags? The man she'd resented for so long *loved* her! And she knew that, yes, she'd forgiven him—almost from day one—though hadn't wanted to admit it!

'But first,' Max murmured, 'I have to know how to end this story.'

Candida waited before answering, trailing her fingers along his strong neck, feeling it tense beneath her touch, then gently pulling him towards her.

With a long, shuddering sigh of relief, Max got up from his knees in one easy movement, and enveloped her in his arms, feeling the soft curves of her body meld with the masculine hardness of his own. Their lips met in the urgent fusing of two people who desired each other, who were meant for each other, and who—at last—understood each other. And this time Candida didn't resist, but allowed herself the intoxicating pleasure of feeling his lusty maleness against her. She *was* dreaming, she thought. Such ecstasy didn't belong here on earth! How could everything have been resolved, she wondered, without any help from *her*? But of course she *knew* how! Her guardian angel had been there beside her all along—not only arranging for her to fall in love with the most handsome, incredible man in the world, but giving her a real opportunity to take up her pen again!

Suddenly she tensed. Wasn't this all too good to be true?

'I don't think that it is me you want, Max,' she said slowly. 'Think about it. Could we really be happy together?' Though even as she uttered those words Candida knew that *she'd* have no problem! She could be content with him for ever! But Max…? Would one female be enough for him? Especially someone like her?

'The circles you move in, the women you mix with,' she went on. 'I am not like them, Max, and I could never be. Would never *want* to be anyone other than myself.' She looked up at him, a slight frown crossing her features. 'I will never change for anyone, Max. I will never change in order to suit someone else's expectations—'

'Precisely so,' he interrupted smoothly. 'And that is why I am perfectly satisfied that it *is* you I want to spend the rest of my days with.' He paused. 'Just consider this,' he went on. 'Who else would quarrel with me about my characters' motives? Who else would tell me off about the endings I choose?' He smiled into her eyes. 'And who else would come blackberrying with me every autumn?'

He closed his lips gently over hers again, and Candida melted once more into the protective closeness of him, thinking that she wouldn't mind staying like this for ever! In her wildest and most imaginative dreams nothing could exceed this—her first marriage proposal from the most desirable man on the planet! Every woman deserved to feel as she was feeling now, she thought.

She nestled her head into Max's shoulder and he tucked her in protectively, kissing her ear, the nape of her neck, her lips, as if already there wasn't a single part of her that wasn't his to love…to cherish…to adore until the end of their days. This surely was, Candida thought dreamily, her chance of a lifetime!

HARLEQUIN® *Presents*®

Harlequin Presents brings you
a brand-new duet by star author

Sharon Kendrick

THE GREEK BILLIONAIRES' BRIDES

Possessed by two Greek billionaire brothers

Alexandros Pavlidis always ended his affairs before
boredom struck. After a passionate relationship with
Rebecca Gibbs, he never expected to see her again.
Until she arrived at his office—pregnant, with twins!

Don't miss

THE GREEK TYCOON'S CONVENIENT WIFE,

on sale July 2008

REQUEST YOUR FREE BOOKS!

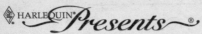

2 FREE NOVELS PLUS 2 FREE GIFTS!

YES! Please send me 2 FREE Harlequin Presents® novels and my 2 FREE gifts (gifts are worth about $10). After receiving them, if I don't wish to receive any more books, I can return the shipping statement marked "cancel". If I don't cancel, I will receive 6 brand-new novels every month and be billed just $4.05 per book in the U.S. or $4.74 per book in Canada, plus 25¢ shipping and handling per book and applicable taxes, if any*. That's a savings of close to 15% off the cover price! I understand that accepting the 2 free books and gifts places me under no obligation to buy anything. I can always return a shipment and cancel at any time. Even if I never buy another book, the two free books and gifts are mine to keep forever.

106 HDN ERRW 306 HDN ERRL

Name	(PLEASE PRINT)	
Address		Apt. #
City	State/Prov.	Zip/Postal Code

Signature (if under 18, a parent or guardian must sign)

Mail to the **Harlequin Reader Service:**
IN U.S.A.: P.O. Box 1867, Buffalo, NY 14240-1867
IN CANADA: P.O. Box 609, Fort Erie, Ontario L2A 5X3

Not valid to current subscribers of Harlequin Presents books.

Want to try two free books from another line?
Call 1-800-873-8635 or visit www.morefreebooks.com.

* Terms and prices subject to change without notice. N.Y. residents add applicable sales tax. Canadian residents will be charged applicable provincial taxes and GST. Offer not valid in Quebec. This offer is limited to one order per household. All orders subject to approval. Credit or debit balances in a customer's account(s) may be offset by any other outstanding balance owed by or to the customer. Please allow 4 to 6 weeks for delivery. Offer available while quantities last.

Your Privacy: Harlequin Books is committed to protecting your privacy. Our Privacy Policy is available online at www.eHarlequin.com or upon request from the Reader Service. From time to time we make our lists of customers available to reputable third parties who may have a product or service of interest to you. If you would prefer we not share your name and address, please check here. ☐

Silhouette®

SPECIAL EDITION™

NEW YORK TIMES BESTSELLING AUTHOR

DIANA PALMER

A brand-new Long, Tall Texans novel

HEART OF STONE

Feeling unwanted and unloved, Keely returns
to Jacobsville and to Boone Sinclair, a rancher
troubled by his own past. Boone has always
seemed reserved, but now Keely discovers a
sensuality with him that quickly turns to love. Can
they each see past their own scars to let love in?

*Available September 2008
wherever you buy books.*